FESTIVAL

THROUGH THE YEAR

STORIES

FESTIVAL
THROUGH THE YEAR
STORIES

Rachna Chhabria

Illustrated by Rayika Sen

HarperCollins*Children'sBooks*

First published in India in 2018 by HarperCollins *Children's Books*
An imprint of HarperCollins *Publishers*
A-75, Sector 57, Noida, Uttar Pradesh 201301, India
www.harpercollins.co.in

4 6 8 10 9 7 5 3
Copyright © Rachna Chhabria 2018
Illustrations © HarperCollins *Publishers* India

P-ISBN: 978-93-5302-352-2

Rachna Chhabria asserts the moral right
to be identified as the author of this work.

While every attempt has been made to authenticate the information
about the festivals included in this book, we apologize for any
unintentional errors or omissions.

Typeset in Garamond, 11.65/16.3 by Sanjeev Kumar

Printed and bound at
Replika Press Pvt. Ltd.

Contents

Prologue   9

1. Celebrating Lohri in the Village   11

2. Dadi's Prize-Winning Pongal Dish   21

3. Kite-Flying on Makar Sankranti   31

4. All Yellow on Vasant Panchami   37

5. Maha Shivratri Blessings   44

6. Being Smart on Holi   51

7. Satheji's Gudi Padwa Invitation   58

8. Good News on Ugadi   65

9. Sarla Aunty's Cheti Chand Treat   72

10. A Gift on Ram Navami   79

11. Dadi's Maun Vrat on Mahavir Jayanti   87

12. A Secret Revealed on Hanuman Jayanti   94

13. VS Egg Hunt on Easter   101

14. Dadu's Bihu Memories   109

15. The Twins' Baisakhi Surprise   115

16. Potluck on Poila Baishak   123

17. Lata's Vishukkani   130

18. Akshaya Tritiya with a Twist   136

19. Passing on the Goodness on Buddha Purnima   143

20. Eid Mubarak, Amina and Arbaaz   150

21. Guru Purnima Quiz with Mrs Rathore   158

22. Master Chef Nikhil's Akuri for Navroz   165

23. Nikhil's Gluttony on Onam   171

24. Raksha Bandhan Surprise for Natasha   183

25. Natasha's Shrikhand for Janmashtami   191

26. Dadi's Ganesh Chaturthi Tales   197

27. Durga Puja and Dandiya on Navratri   203

28. Community Ayudha Puja   210

29. Dussehra Delight   217

30. Diwali with a Difference   223

31. Making Karah Parshad on Gurpurab   231

32. Santas Come Visiting on Christmas   238

*For Dad, Mom
and Amma*

Prologue

Manhattan, America

'Nikhil and Natasha, I need to tell you something,' their mother said.

Exchanging a look, the twins moved close to each other. Even their dog, Bruno, a fawn-coloured Dobermann, watched their parents silently, as though awaiting a major revelation. Ten-year-old Nikhil was thin and fair, with a round face and a wide forehead. A mop of wayward, black hair, which he combed only before leaving for school, crowned his head. Natasha, his twin sister, younger to him by fifteen minutes, was thin and fair like her brother, with large eyes, a small face and two freckles that stood out on her button-like nose. Her shoulder-length black hair was tied in a ponytail. Their mother, Anita Kapoor, was an older version of Natasha; they looked so alike.

'Your father and I have decided that this is the right time for both of us to relocate to India. We have already informed our companies that we would like to return to our country. Luckily for us, your Christmas vacations are on, so this is the perfect time to take you to India, to your grandparents' house.'

The twins were silent.

Bruno sat down on his hind legs. Turning to the twins, his tail upright, he barked softly, as though saying, 'Oh no.'

'We have got you both admitted in an elite school in Bengaluru,' their dad, Aman Kapoor, added. Nikhil closely resembled his dad,

the only difference being that his father combed his hair more often than Nikhil did!

'Though you have missed out on several months' syllabus in school, your grandmother has assured me that she will help you catch up with the missed portions in school by way of extra classes and special coaching,' their mother said.

'We are leaving for India in three days,' their father said and smiled. 'After you both settle down in my parents' house, your mom and I will return to America.'

'We think it's the right time for you two to move back to India so you can connect with your roots. We don't want you to miss out on all the culture and traditions that make India what it is.'

'What if we can't adjust?' Natasha asked.

'You will,' their mom replied.

'What about Bruno?' she asked.

'He will stay with us.'

'Can't we go later, with you?' Nikhil asked. 'We will be on an airplane on our birthday?'

'Start packing,' their dad said, in a gentle yet firm voice.

1

Celebrating Lohri
in the Village

The crackling flames leapt upwards in the light of the setting Sun. Tears rolled down Natasha's cheeks as she stared at the bonfire that her grandmother Harmeet Kapoor's brother had lit in the backyard of his large farmhouse in rural Punjab. Her heart twisted with pain as memories of America and her parents jostled each other in her mind. She and her twin brother were now staying in Bengaluru, with their paternal grandparents, who wanted to be called Dadu and Dadi and not grandpa and grandma.

Natasha wiped away her tears. She missed her friends, her dog Bruno and their house in Manhattan. She and her brother had celebrated their eleventh birthday in December in the plane. Adjusting to the Indian climate hadn't been easy for Natasha. But her sibling had taken an instant liking to India, adjusting so fast that it seemed as though he had been born and brought up here. Now, it was nearly three weeks since the twins had landed in the country of their parent's birth – a place they had only visited twice before.

Since they had arrived only late last year, Lohri was the first festival they were celebrating.

Natasha looked up as Dadi put her arm around her and hugged her tight. 'You miss your life in America, don't you?' she said softly. Dadi was a sprightly lady, tall and well-built, with thick salt-and-pepper hair tied in a single plait, which touched the base of her backbone. She had translucent skin, untouched by wrinkles or spots. She always wore salwar suits, with her dupatta pinned neatly at her shoulders. Her round-frame glasses suited her; she had frames of different colours and liked to match these to her outfits.

Pushing his glasses up, Dadu moved his chair closer to Natasha. A warm smile appeared on his square face, as he looked at her fondly. His eyes always had a hint of laughter in them, and his dusky skin glowed with health. Holding her hand in his, he said, 'I'm sure you will soon settle down so well in India that you will forget America.'

She shivered as a sudden gust of wind swept over them, leaving Dadu's thick, grey hair in disarray.

'Your parents always wanted you and Nikhil to spend Lohri in the village, but sadly, because of their work schedule, they could never bring you here during the time of the festival.' Dadi's eyes were moist. 'But I'm glad that in a year or two, they too will come to India permanently. Your dad went to America to study engineering and met your mom in college. The two came back to India to get married but then returned there to work.'

'Lohri is a lot like what Americans celebrate as Thanksgiving,' Dadu changed the topic as he could see his wife getting nostalgic and tearful.

'Dadu, wait,' Natasha said, pulling out her journal and pen from the handbag at her feet. 'I want to keep a journal of all the Indian festivals and the myths associated with them. Can you please give me the details of this festival?'

'Sure,' Dadu said, making his plump frame comfortable in the chair. 'But first, let's follow the rituals. Then I'll give you the details.'

'Can you believe that Lohri typically falls on the same date every year—the 13th of January—much like Christmas?' Dadi said, her eyes twinkling in the glow of the fire. 'And it is observed the night before Makar Sankranti, which is also called Maghi.'

'Wow,' Natasha said. 'I had no idea! The dates of most Indian festivals keep changing. I remember we would celebrate the same festivals on different dates every year, back in the States.'

'By celebrating, you mean wearing your traditional clothes and meeting your parents' Indian friends for potluck?' Dadi snorted.

Dadu laughed, stretching his long legs as he clasped his hands behind his head. 'Lohri signifies the successful harvest of the winter crop season. People also thank Surya devta, the Sun God. As farmers are so dependent on the elements of nature, they worship nature.'

Natasha scribbled furiously in her journal.

'In Punjab, one of the Lohri traditions is to eat sheaves of roasted corn from the new harvest, as well as the January sugarcane harvest and groundnuts.'

Natasha picked up a piece of sugarcane from a plate on the table close by and popped it into her mouth.

'Earlier, as part of Lohri celebrations, children went around their neighbourhood singing the traditional folk songs of Lohri. I remember my grandmother telling me, when I was young, that while one child sang the folk song, the other children screamed "ho" at the end of each line. After the song was over, the people whose house the children were visiting were expected to give the kids snacks and a treat.' Chewing on a small piece of sugarcane, Dadi continued, 'No one turned away the children empty-handed as it was considered inauspicious. And if a family was celebrating something auspicious, like a marriage or the birth of a baby, then the children demanded even more treats.' Discarding her chewed piece of sugarcane into a paper napkin, she smiled. 'My own grandmother would go around singing the folk songs while her siblings joined in with the refrain of "ho".'

Natasha, too, threw away her chewed piece of sugarcane.

Dadu took over. 'The collection amassed by the children is known as *Lohri,* which comprises til, gajak, crystal sugar, gur, peanuts, popcorn and candies. If the household is in a celebratory mood, the children get some money too. At night, this *Lohri* is divided equally among the children.'

'Oh, just like the trick-or-treating we did during Halloween,' Natasha said excitedly.

'Yes,' her grandparents laughed.

'Try these,' Dadi said, picking up a large plate from a table beside her. 'I made these two chikkis – one of them has gur and groundnuts, which I roasted over the fire to make it crisp, and the other has gur and til, which you know as sesame seeds.'

'Gur or jaggery chikkis are more tasty and healthy than the ones made with sugar,' Nikhil chimed in and grabbed a handful to pop into his mouth.

'Yes, Master Chef Nikhil, who else but you will know that,' Dadi said, grinning. She ruffled his wayward hair fondly and hugged her grandson.

'Now both of you can join me and your Dadu as we go around the fire.' She picked up a handful of sesame seeds, gur and rewaries to throw into the fire.

Natasha and Nikhil followed their grandparents as they circled the fire and threw the offering into the dancing flames.

'You can also chant any prayer you know while going around the fire,' Dadi instructed. 'This is to pay your respects to the natural element of fire, which is a common tradition during any winter-solstice celebration. Throwing food into the fire also represents the burning of the old year and the start of the next one on Makar Sankranti.'

Like her grandparents, Natasha circled the fire three times and threw the food into the flames with her right hand. She watched the flames leap up and devour the offerings.

A few people had started beating the dhol—a kind of drum—which was decorated with colourful tassels. Her

aunts, uncles and cousins danced around the fire to the beat of the dhol.

Natasha grinned when she saw Nikhil trying to learn the Gidda. For someone born and brought up in Manhattan, he seemed to be managing quite well. Her aunt set the long table, which had been brought out into the backyard from the living room. Natasha's mouth watered at the sight of the traditional food: piping hot sarson ka saag, makki ki roti, gajak, and small chunks of gur. There was also tricholi, or til rice, made by mixing jaggery, sesame seeds and rice.

'This sarson ka saag is a lot like spinach, but it's more flavourful. And the large amount of butter gives it a smooth texture,' Nikhil said, shoving a big piece of the makki ki roti—with which he had scooped up the green vegetable—into his mouth. 'Must ask Dadi to teach me how to make this.' He sighed contentedly, licking his fingers.

'I've started my journal,' Natasha said. 'I'll make notes about the festivals we will celebrate.'

'Copycat,' Nikhil said, making a face. 'You are lifting my idea of a blog.'

Leaving her grandparents chatting with other relatives, Natasha scribbled in her journal.

Natasha's Journal

*This is my first Lohri. This Punjabi folk festival, celebrated on
13 January, has such a musical name. This festival celebrates the
passing of the winter solstice, the end of the winter season and
the Sun's journey to the northern hemisphere. With the arrival of
Lohri, the days become longer and the nights shorter.*

*The Lohri tradition requires the lighting of a bonfire in one's
backyard. People sing and dance around the fire to mark the end of
winter and the harvesting of the rabi or winter crop.*

*Dulla Bhatti's name figures in many Lohri folk songs. According
to Lohri folklore, Dulla Bhatti, whose real name was Abdullah
Bhatti, lived in Punjab during the reign of Mughal Emperor
Akbar. He was considered a hero, but he also had a Robin Hood
image and is said to have robbed the rich to feed the poor during the
Mughal period. It's believed that he rescued Hindu girls from being
abducted and sold into slavery in the Middle East. Amongst the
girls he saved were two called Sundri and Mundri, who, for some
reason, became a theme in Punjabi folklore. Maybe because their
names rhymed and were easy to remember.*

*Dadi said that some people believe that the name Lohri is derived
from Loi, who was the wife of Sant Kabir, because in some parts
of Punjab, people pronounce Lohri as Lohi. Even Dadi pronounced
it as Lohi. Among the many legends associated with the festival is
the one of two sisters, Holika and Lohri. While Holika burnt in
the Holi fire, Lohri survived. Dadi said that some people make an*

image of the Lohri Goddess with cow dung, which she called 'gobar'. The image is then decorated and a fire lit beneath it, and songs in praise of the Goddess are sung around the fire.

During Lohri, people usually have private celebrations in their homes, where they perform the rituals of the festival around the fire. Singing and dancing are an important part of this festival. I noticed that everyone was wearing bright clothes and doing the Bhangra and Gidda to the beat of the dhol or to popular songs. They were all just letting their hair down.

Sarson ka saag and makki ki roti are usually served as the main course at a Lohri dinner. Sugarcane, groundnuts, til, radish, corn, mustard greens and gur are all important ingredients of the Lohri feast. I ate quite a lot of gur, but Nikhil ate much more than me!

For the farmers, Lohri is a very important festival. However, people residing in towns and cities also celebrate it, as it provides an opportunity to revel with family and friends.

Dadu told me that the Sindhi community celebrates this festival too, but they call it Lal Loi. According to the Sindhi custom, family and friends sing and dance around a fire and burn their individual wooden sticks in it. Dadi said even milk and water is poured around the bonfire to thank the Sun God and seek his blessings.

Living with Dadu and Dadi is not as bad as I had thought it would be. Both are quite chilled out, though Dadi is high on discipline. Dadi and Dadu had met in school. Dadu is a Punjabi, and Dadi a Sardarni. I love the idea that they were childhood friends. As Dadu was in the army (one of his friends from the army still calls him Brigadier), he and Dadi were posted in many states. This is one of the reasons why they are so familiar with the festivals and the food of so many different states in India. And, of course, it helps that Dadi loves to cook.

Dadi's family is a cosmopolitan one. Her younger sister married into an Assamese family, while her younger brother married into a Gujarati one. Only her elder brother and elder sister were married into Sikh families.

2

Dadi's Prize-Winning Pongal Dish

Nikhil woke up to the soothing sound of his Dadi's soft voice singing the morning aarti, accompanied by the puja bell. He peered sleepily at the alarm beside him on the dresser: 5:30 a.m.

'Oh no,' he moaned, 'I'm late!' After last night's revelry, he could do with a few more hours of sleep. But Dadi had asked him to join her for some ritual. Nikhil darted into the bathroom. Twenty minutes later, as he was hurriedly combing his wayward hair, he heard the house bell ring. His sixty-two-year-old Dadi had won India's Innovative Chef Award two weeks back, and life had not been the same ever since. For one, Dadi had been flooded with requests for interviews and appearances on chat shows; for another, there was a constant stream of visitors and phone calls, not just in Bengaluru but even now, while they were holidaying in Punjab. And as Dadi's self-appointed secretary-cum-assistant, Nikhil's workload had increased.

The unique taste of Dadi's recipes had won over the judges and left them amazed at how innovative each one was. Her Baked Pongal Cheesecake recipe had bagged the one lakh rupee prize. And after news had leaked out that she was the creator of the recipe blog 'Grandma's Corner', which Nikhil had helped set up, she had been flooded with comments from food lovers all over the world. Dadi had become an overnight celebrity. She had even been approached by a television channel to host her own cookery show, and a couple of newspapers were hounding her to write a column for them.

'I wish Dadi hadn't declined all the offers,' Nikhil muttered. 'It would have been nice to see her host her own cookery show.'

'Talking to oneself is the first sign of madness,' Natasha said, with a wide smile. She stood in the doorway, holding the brass bell that had accompanied Dadi's bhajan. 'Hurry up, will you,' she said impatiently, 'the cows won't wait forever.'

Sliding his feet into his slippers, Nikhil ran out of the room, following his sister.

In the backyard, two large mud pots were simmering over burning logs of wood. Five bricks surrounded the burning logs on three sides to make a temporary wall. The gentle aroma of cardamom wafted out of one pot and that of pure ghee out of the other.

'Ah,' Dadi sighed contentedly, as the rice boiled over the side of both the pots.

'Dadi, the rice is spilling over,' Natasha said.

'Tradition says this rice should boil or spill over,' Dadi said with a smile. 'In Tamil, the word *Pongal* means "overflowing", signifying abundance and prosperity. Do you know that today is Pongal?'

Natasha looked puzzled. 'I thought "pongal" was the name of a rice dish – the same dish that won you the prize.'

'The people of Tamil Nadu celebrate the festival of Pongal by eating pongal,' Dadi said. 'Pongal is a dish as well as the name of a popular festival. In fact, the festival is so popular that the entire state of Tamil Nadu practically comes to a halt at Pongal time. If you visit Tamil Nadu during this time, you will see deserted roads, and if you are lucky, like I was, you will see decorated cattle.'

'The sweet pongal made specially in earthenware pots over a wood fire tastes delicious,' Nikhil said, smacking his lips. When he saw his sister looking at him with raised eyebrows, he added, 'I read it on the internet. It's called chakkara pongal and is usually prepared in temples as prasad. We can also use white sugar instead of gur, right, Dadi?' he asked.

Stirring the pot with a wooden ladle, Dadi nodded, deep in thought. 'It is a tradition to make sweet pongal on

Pongal, but I have made the savoury version as well, since my family wanted to taste both.'

'Where is everybody?' Nikhil asked.

'On the terrace,' Dadi said, 'getting ready to fly kites as we are leaving in the afternoon for Bengaluru.'

'What is this festival about?' Natasha asked, turning to a new page in her journal.

'You mother is half-Tamil! Don't tell me you've never celebrated Pongal?' Dadi said.

Natasha's face turned red.

'First the rituals, please,' Dadi said, as she added chopped cashews into the two pots.

The watchman led a cow and a buffalo into the backyard.

'Early this morning, while you were sleeping, I painted the horns of the buffalo,' Dadi said, pointing to the colourful horns. She had made circles of different colours on the buffalo's horns. 'Don't worry, I used natural dyes,' she assured the twins.

Lifting two garlands of flowers from a thali beside her, she handed them to the children. 'Worshipping cows is an integral part of the Pongal festival, and luckily for us, my brother's watchman brought us the buffalo.'

Nikhil quickly garlanded the cow.

'Dadi, what if he kicks me?' Natasha said, moving towards the buffalo reluctantly.

'He won't,' Dadi replied. 'Just garland him fast.'

Putting the garland quickly around the buffalo's neck, Natasha moved back, scared that it would bite her. She could hear Dadi and Nikhil laughing.

'Boiling of the first rice of the season is one of the major traditions of Pongal. This rice is dedicated to the Sun in a ritual called Surya Mangalyam. In olden times, cooking was done in the sunlight—usually in a porch, backyard or the courtyard—as the dish is dedicated to the Sun God,' Dadi said, as she ladled the rice dish onto banana leaves cut into small squares. Thinking it was for him, Nikhil extended his hand.

'No, the first offering is for the Sun God,' Dadi said. Then she raised her face upwards to look at the Sun, closed her eyes and said a prayer.

The twins did the same.

'Now you two can eat,' Dadi said and placed a small helping of both dishes on the banana leaves. The three of them sat down to eat their breakfast.

'It's delicious,' Nikhil said. He had devoured his share. 'Can I have more?' he asked. 'The fresh air of the countryside is making me hungry.'

'You are always hungry,' Natasha grinned.

'After breakfast, go to the terrace,' Dadi said, serving him a more-than-generous helping of both the sweet and the savoury pongal.

Nikhil's Nook

Hi,

I'm Nikhil Kapoor.

I was born in Manhattan. My parents, who are both Indians (Dad's father is Punjabi and mother a Sikh, and mom has a Punjabi father and Tamil mother), decided to uproot their ten-year-

old children from America and replant them in India, so that we could learn about our culture. After the initial misgivings, I was all for it, though my twin sister, Natasha, grumbled about this move.

As my parents want me to learn about my culture and traditions, I decided to start a blog to write about the festivals I celebrate and the food associated with each festival. (I am specially looking forward to the latter!) Pongal is both a food as well as a festival. This amazing rice dish comes in two versions. The sweet version—made with milk and jaggery and garnished with cashews—is called chakkara pongal and is brownish in colour because of the jaggery. The salty pongal—called ven or khara pongal—is a lighter shade of yellow, because of the yellow lentil. It is laced with cashews and is also a popular tiffin item – by tiffin, I mean breakfast. Piping hot khara pongal is served in practically every restaurant in Tamil Nadu and many places in South India.

During the second week of January, Tamilians celebrate Pongal, also called Thai Pongal (a four-day harvest festival). The Pongal festival is dedicated to the Sun God as a symbol of appreciation for a successful harvest. The day marks the start of the Uttarayan or the Sun's six-month-long journey northwards.

The day preceding Thai Pongal (which is the main day of the festival) is called Bhogi. This day is celebrated in honour of Lord Indra (the god of rain and thunder and the lord of heaven), and farmers seek his blessings for an abundant harvest. The Bhogi ritual is observed on this day. I found this ritual both unique and practical. As part of the ritual, useless household items are tossed *into a bonfire made of cow-dung cakes and wood. In this way, people can rid their houses of useless clutter. People clean their houses thoroughly, with some even painting them for the festival. There is also a ceremony in which the fruits of the harvest such as regi pallu or the jujuba fruit (which Dadi called ber) and sugarcane are gathered along with the seasonal flowers.*

The main event is known as Thai Pongal. It takes place on the second day of the four-day festival. This day coincides with Makar Sankranti. On Thai Pongal day, a special ritual is performed, in which rice and milk and a piece of the turmeric plant are boiled together in an earthen pot out in the open, as an offering to the Sun God. (Nowadays, this ritual is often performed inside the house, as not everyone has backyards.) In addition, sticks of sugarcane, coconuts and bananas are also offered to Surya Devta (as Dadi calls the Sun God). Tamilians decorate their houses with banana and mango leaves, both of which are considered auspicious. Using a paste made of rice powder, they draw intricate handmade patterns— also known as kolams or rangolis—on the doorstep of the house, to welcome Goddess Lakshmi, who is believed to bring prosperity and happiness into the house.

Maatu Pongal is celebrated the day after Thai Pongal. On this day, cattle are worshipped as Tamilians regard them as a source of wealth – cattle help plough the fields, help in transportation and provide dairy products. The cattle are adorned with bells, sheaves of corn and garlands. Legend has it that Lord Shiva sent his bull Basava to Earth with a message for humans, asking them to have an oil massage and bath daily and to eat once a month. The bull got the message mixed up and conveyed to the people that Lord Shiva had asked them to eat daily and have an oil bath once a month. This made Lord Shiva very angry, and he banished Basava to Earth with a curse that he would have to plough the fields to help people produce more food as the people had begun eating more due to Basava's mistake. Hence, this day is associated with cattle.

Kanu or Kannum Pongal marks the last day of Pongal. On this day, a ritual called Kanu Pidi is performed, wherein the leftover sweet pongal and other food, like cooked vegetables and bananas, are set out in the courtyard or on the roof of the house, on ginger and turmeric leaves, for crows and other birds. Women perform this ritual for their brothers, as it is believed that it wards away evil and makes them prosper.

I forgot to mention that there are two more varieties of pongal. That doubles the fun for a foodie like me! Milagu pongal is a spicy version, in which pepper, jeera and moong dal are added to the rice, and in puli pongal, tamarind is added. These dishes have no connection with the Pongal festival and are often eaten for lunch or dinner. I'm hoping Dadi will make both these versions soon.

I enjoyed the cow worship, though my scared sister was worried about the buffalo kicking her. Here's a small secret! I had quickly garlanded the cow, so that the more frightening-looking buffalo was left for her! Next time, I would like to paint their horns.

Before I forget, I must tell you about the dish—Baked Pongal Cheesecake—which won Dadi the Innovative Chef Award. This *cheesecake had a base of groundnuts, til and gur, to which Dadi had added a thin layer of sweet pongal and topped it off with a thick layer of rabri, before setting it to bake. It was delicious. No wonder it won the prize.*

3

Kite-Flying on
Makar Sankranti

The twins rushed up to the terrace, where preparations were underway for the kite-flying contest. Natasha lifted a plain red kite from the pile of colourful kites lying on the table. It was rhombus shaped and made of light-weight paper and bamboo. Turning it around, she saw that it had a central spine and a single bow.

Natasha's cousin Rohan then made four holes in the kite with the precision of a skilled surgeon – two on top, at the crossbar, and two halfway down the spine. He inserted a long piece of string called manjha (the sharp thread with which a kite is flown) into the holes. He then made several knots to hold the string in place, before tying it to the roll of manjha.

The kites on the table fluttered in the wind. But, Natasha was more worried that the wind would carry away her skinny relative. Rohan was all bones, with a long face, a pointed chin and large eyes that looked as though he was constantly surprised. He frequently ran his bony fingers through his thick hair.

Natasha watched Rohan carefully as he tested the string of the kite, before handing it to her and taking the roll of manjha himself.

'Stand away from the wind,' he instructed. 'And make the kite airborne.'

'Thank you, Bhaiya,' Natasha said. Standing with her back to the wind, Natasha watched as her kite became airborne and then, buffeted by the wind, rose higher and higher.

'Here you go,' said Rohan, handing her the roll of manjha. 'Either reel in your line to bring the kite close to you or loosen the string to let it fly higher.'

Natasha watched with delight as her kite took to the skies.

Suddenly, Rohan screamed, 'Reel it in,' as another kite from the neighbouring terrace moved towards her kite.

Natasha rapidly rolled the manjha,

bringing the kite lower and lower. When the other kite moved away, she loosened her string once more. But no sooner was her kite flying high once again than a green kite swayed crazily towards it.

'Reel it in,' Rohan shouted in alarm, racing towards her from the other side of the terrace.

But it was too late. Nikhil, the owner of the green kite, had expertly cut her string.

'Oh no,' Natasha groaned, as her kite flew away into the distance.

'You want me to set up another one for you?' Rohan asked.

'No, I'm done,' she said sadly, before sitting down on a chair to watch the others fly their kites.

Then, pulling out her journal, she started to write.

Natasha's Journal

Today, I flew my first kite to celebrate Makar Sankranti, or Makara Sankranti as some people call it. This festival is dedicated to Surya, the Sun God; people pray to him and thank him for their success and prosperity. This festival also marks the beginning of a six-month auspicious period for Hindus – the Uttarayan period, which signals the arrival of longer days and spring. Most festivals follow the lunar cycle. Makar Sankranti is one of the few ancient Indian festivals that is observed according to the solar cycle, which is also why it almost always falls on the same Gregorian date (Dadu told me that the Gregorian calendar is the most widely used civil calendar in the world) every year – 14 January. In some rare instances, the date might shift by a day owing to the movement of the Earth and the Sun, which, to be honest, confused me.

I was surprised to learn that Makar Sankranti is a pan-India solar festival and that it is known by different names throughout India. It's called Maghi by North Indian Hindus and Sikhs, Makara Sankranti in Karnataka, Pedda Panduga in Andhra Pradesh, Sukarat in Central India, Magh Bihu in Assam, Uttarayan in Gujarat and Pongal in Tamil Nadu. For most parts of India, this period marks the early stages of the rabi crop and the crop cycle, where crops have been sown and the work in the fields is almost over. So, this is a time for rejoicing and celebrations.

This festival is celebrated with melas and fairs. People sing and dance around bonfires. Sadly, we couldn't attend a mela as we had to leave for the airport.

Dadi told me that in the rural areas, children often go from house to house during Makar Sankranti, singing and asking for treats.

I noticed something: though Makar Sankranti is celebrated differently in various parts of India, one thing is common in all the traditions, and that is the making of sticky sweets, especially with sesame and gur.

Interestingly, Dadi told me that a Harvard University professor specializing in Indology had discovered that Magha mela (melas held during the Magha festival) have been mentioned in the Mahabharata. This means that this festival has been around for a very long time.

On this auspicious day, people also take a dip in rivers and lakes that are sacred to them while thanking the Sun. Kumbh Mela, one of the largest pilgrimages that occurs once every twelve years, falls on Makar Sankranti and is held at the confluence of two rivers, Ganga and Yamuna.

Uttarayan is symbolized by the flying of kites in Gujarat. The International Kite Festival takes place in Ahmedabad, which is called the Kite Capital of Gujarat. Scores of people from all over the country as well as from abroad come to participate in this annual festival. Preparations begin months in advance. I read that the best place to enjoy this festival is the Sabarmati River. The Sabarmati River bank has the capacity to accommodate a large crowd.

Rohan Bhaiya, who is from Ahmedabad, told me that in the week leading up to the festival, the Patang Bazar, in the heart of Ahmedabad, is open around the clock. Dadu told me that when he was posted in Ahmedabad, he had seen many households that made kites at home, setting up small shops inside their house or garage. He had also taken Dadi to the Kite Museum, which was established in 1985 at Sanskar Kendra in the Paldi area of Ahmedabad. Rohan Bhaiya showed me pictures of the unique kites in the museum.

Though my first attempt at flying kites did not go too well, I wouldn't mind trying again. I've decided that after the exams are over, I'll ask Dadu to teach me how to fly a kite.

Dadi thinks kite-flying is also beneficial for health. She says that the Sun's rays in the early morning are an excellent source of Vitamin D and are good for the skin and bones.

Two of Uttarayan's most popular local dishes are undhiyu and jalebis. Undhiyu is a mixed-vegetable dish that includes yam, potatoes, peas, sweet potato, unripe banana, beans and methi ki muthiya or fried fenugreek dumplings. Dadi made undhiyu last week. It was so delicious that I had three helpings. That day, I could easily have beaten Nikhil in gluttony, if he hadn't eaten more jalebis than I did!

4

All Yellow on
Vasant Panchami

'Achoo,' Dadi sneezed. She had sneezed fifteen times in the last hour. A pile of paper napkins littered the dresser, next to which she sat blowing her nose every few minutes. Her eyes watered, and her nose had turned red and begun to flake. She was quite a sight! Natasha looked worriedly at her grandmother. Soon after they had returned from Punjab, Dadi had caught a cold, which had turned into a viral infection.

Her usually genial grandmother had become a grouch, constantly finding fault with everything.

'The soup was too spicy, the pepper irritated my throat,' Dadi told Lata.

Lata, the Kapoors' cook-cum-housekeeper, looked miffed at the comment. She stood stiffly next to Dadi's bed in her beige cotton sari, a picture of disappointment. When she turned around to lift the empty soup bowl, her curly hair captured in a tight plait came within inches of Dadi's nose.

'Don't stand too close to me. Your hair oil is irritating my sinus,' Dadi said.

Lata's face fell.

'Why is your coat on the sofa?' Dadi asked Dadu, vexedly. 'It won't walk into the cupboard by itself.'

Dadu mumbled something in reply. Then, picking up his mobile phone from the bed, he exclaimed, 'Oh, I was supposed to meet Mehta in the park.' Waving a hasty goodbye, he darted out of the room.

'Madam, you are inviting more germs by keeping the soiled tissues so close to yourself,' Lata chided her mistress gently. Sweeping the pile of used napkins into a dustbin, she swept out of the room.

'Lata has become unbearable,' Dadi grumbled. Natasha tried to suppress her giggle. The same could be said of her grandmother.

'Yeah,' Nikhil nodded, sitting in Dadu's rocking chair and typing something on his laptop.

'Lata!' Dadi screamed. The housekeeper rushed into the room with a fearful look on her face.

'Now what, Madam, is the tea not to your taste?'

'No need to act so smart,' Dadi remarked. 'I hope you remembered to make the right food today?'

'Yes,' Lata said proudly. 'Today I've outdone myself. Even

a super cook like you will be proud of me.'

'I hope so,' Dadi sniffled. 'You have become absent-minded nowadays. I had asked you to get me the newspaper. But you forgot.'

Lata stared pointedly at the newspaper lying beside the bed.

Dadi turned to look. Seeing the paper lying there, she exclaimed, 'Oh, you must have kept it there when I nodded off to sleep.'

'I gave it to you in your hand, but I guess this cold has made you a bit absent-minded,' Lata grinned.

'Never mind,' Dadi said crossly.

'I need to go back to the kitchen,' Lata said, as she hurried out of the room.

Dadi turned to look at the twins. Natasha was wearing a yellow one-piece dress, and Nikhil wore a yellow t-shirt over faded blue jeans. 'For a change, you two have worn the right colours today,' she said approvingly.

'Meaning?' Nikhil frowned.

Before their grandmother could reply, Lata entered the room. 'Madam, I've kept everything ready for Saraswati Puja,' she said.

'Finally you did something right, Lata dear.' Dadi made a face. 'Follow me into the puja room,' she said. 'I'll supervise the Saraswati Puja for you both.'

Nikhil and Natasha followed Dadi into the small

prayer room, where idols of gods and goddesses sat on different shelves.

Draped in yellow-coloured silk, Goddess Saraswati sat on a lotus with a veena in her hand. 'Lata loves making clothes for my gods,' Dadi said, pleasure evident in her voice. 'There is a story behind each of the idols, but I'll tell you those stories some other day.'

Following Dadi's instructions, Nikhil and Natasha placed a yellow marigold at the goddess's feet. Then, dipping their fourth finger in the bowl of sandalwood paste that Lata had kept in the puja room, they applied a small tilak on the goddess's head and added a little kumkum from a small silver katori over the sandalwood mark. The kheer Lata had made was offered to the goddess.

'Ask for Goddess Saraswati's blessings,' Dadi said. Joining their palms, the twins bowed their heads. 'She

is the goddess of learning. Both of you badly need her blessings. I saw your marks in the weekly tests. Your Maths marks were pathetic,' she scowled at Nikhil. Then, turning to Natasha, she added, 'And your Biology and Chemistry scores were no better.'

Lata announced lunch before Dadi could grumble some more. They trooped into the dining room, sniffing appreciatively.

Lata had made lemon rice, gatte ki sabzi, dhokla, yellow dal and sweet boondi. For dessert, she served them piping hot kheer made with crushed rice grains, into which she had added some saffron to give it a yellow colour. She had also made pumpkin halwa and bought jalebis from the sweet shop down the road.

'The kheer looks delicious, Lata didi,' Nikhil said.

'Wow!' Natasha exclaimed. 'Looks like the food theme is yellow today.'

'Yes,' Dadi said, serving herself a helping of lemon rice. 'All the dishes look good, Lata,' she said.

'Thank you, Madam,' the housekeeper smiled, relieved to see that Dadi's mood had improved!

Nikhil's Nook

Hi Friends,

I'm back to celebrate another festival.

Vasant Panchami, also spelled as Basant Panchami, marks the arrival of spring. I had no idea that Vasant Panchami has a specific meaning: Vasant means 'spring' and Panchami means 'the fifth day'. So, Vasant Panchami means the fifth day of spring. Also known as Shree Panchami, it is celebrated every year on the fifth day of the month of Magha, which typically falls in late January or February. Vasant Panchami is dedicated to Goddess Saraswati – the goddess of knowledge, language, music and the arts. It is believed that Goddess Saraswati symbolizes creative energy and power in all its forms. She is, therefore, the inspiration for artists from different fields.

Vasant Panchami also symbolizes the ripening of the mustard crop with its yellow flowers. Yellow is considered Saraswati's favourite colour, and so, the festival is associated with this colour. People dress in yellow clothes on this day. I was surprised to learn that people also eat yellow-coloured snacks and sweets on this day! They add saffron to their rice to give it a yellow colour. And the Vasant Panchami feast has a yellow food theme. Many families initiate infants and young children into learning on Vasant Panchami day by making them write their first words with their index fingers in a thali filled with grain. Students keep their pens, textbooks and notebooks at the feet of the Saraswati idol to seek her blessings.

Temples and educational institutions drape statues of Saraswati in yellow clothes and offer yellow flowers to the goddess. Many educational institutions and music and dance academies organize special prayers or pujas in the morning to seek the blessings of the goddess. Poetry recitations, dance programmes and musical shows are held in some communities and schools.

On Vasant Panchami, yellow sweets such as besan laddoos, jalebis, kheer laced with saffron, sweet boondi, boondi laddoos and mysore pak are offered to Goddess Saraswati.

I'm just wondering, can a budding chef (oops, my secret is out!) pray to Goddess Saraswati? I feel all kinds of creativity needs her grace. I'm glad that my Saraswati Puja was so simple and easy, because I'm going to do it every year.

5

Maha Shivratri Blessings

'Lord Shiva already gave us his blessings,' Natasha grinned.

'What do you mean?' Her brother frowned.

The siblings were sitting in Nikhil's bedroom, ready for the day. Nikhil was on his laptop, while Natasha was reading a book.

'Didn't he get us out of the jagran—the all-night prayer and bhajan-singing session—that Dadi wanted to drag us to last night at her friend's house?' Natasha said.

'Yeah,' Nikhil nodded. 'Though I love Lord Shiva, I don't think I am up for an all-night vigil,' he said softly.

'Why are you whispering?' Natasha asked.

'I don't want Dadi to feel bad that we weren't interested in the jagran,' he said. 'Thank God Dadu put his foot down, or else we would have had to put up with Sarla Aunty's offkey singing. She doesn't have a single musical bone in her body. I'm sure her singing can even scare away ghosts.'

'Where did you hear her singing?'

'Last week, Dadi sent me on an errand to Sarla Aunty's house. Her housekeeper asked me to wait in the living room as aunty was praying. I nearly jumped up from the sofa in alarm when I heard her sing a bhajan. Her shrill voice felt like a hundred doors creaking in protest. I saw the housekeeper stuffing her ears with cotton,' said Nikhil. 'I asked her to lend me some,' he added, grinning widely at the memory.

'You really asked her for cotton?' Natasha asked with a smile.

'Yeah, I had no intention of going deaf,' he replied.

'But we have to go to her house to offer milk to Lord Shiva,' she said.

'That won't be a problem as I doubt she will sing today,' he said.

'Children, see what I got you from the market,' Dadi entered the room carrying a cloth bag. She pulled out two japamalas of rudraksha beads. 'For you both,' she said, handing each of them a japamala.

'Wow!' Natasha caressed her beads. The even-sized prayer beads with similar markings looked pretty. 'Thanks, Dadi, this is an amazing rudraksha mala.'

'Each mala has 108 beads. Hold the mala in your right hand. Chant *Om Namah Shivaya* at every bead. When you reach the meru or head bead, which is the top part of the japamala, you will have completed one mala. You can then turn it around and start your second mala,' Dadi instructed. 'And I forgot to tell you, Sarla has invited us for the Maha Shivratri puja. Don't worry, she won't sing any bhajans today.' Dadi's eyes twinkled.

Nikhil blushed. 'You heard us?'

'Try chanting the mantra I have just taught you while I get ready.' Their grandmother walked out of the room, closing the door softly behind her.

Sitting cross-legged on her brother's bed, Natasha lifted the mala in her right hand. She closed her eyes and started chanting the mantra that their Dadi had just taught them. She had completed three malas when she heard the door open.

When Natasha opened her eyes, she saw Dadi standing there wearing a green salwar-kurta, her dupatta neatly pinned at her shoulders.

'Let's go,' she said.

The twins accompanied her two floors down to the Sadhwanis' house. Sarla Aunty and Sushil Uncle were their grandparents' best friends. Removing their slippers outside the door, they entered the house. It was packed with Sarla Aunty's family and close friends. The siblings followed their grandmother to the puja room, where Sarla Aunty sat cross-legged on a beige-coloured mat. Though she was slim, she had plump cheeks on a round face and her brown eyes always had a mischievous twinkle in them. She sat beside a high wooden table, on which lay a silver Shiva-Lingam and Nandi inside a small plate.

'Sit down beside me,' Sarla Aunty smiled at them. She handed Natasha a small copper pot—also called a kalash— filled with thandai and asked her to slowly pour it over the Shiva Lingam. Then Natasha observed how she placed a three-leaf clover of bael leaves on the lingam and offered fruits and flowers from a wicker basket kept on the side.

'Don't go without drinking the thandai,' Sarla Aunty said, as they left the puja room.

Sarla Aunty's housekeeper—Bela, a plump girl, prone to giggling—was serving people chilled thandai in long steel glasses. Approaching the twins, the young housekeeper held out the tray to them. As they lifted a glass each, she whispered to Nikhil, 'You want cotton today?'

Nikhil quickly averted his gaze.

Natasha's Journal

Though thandai is a traditional Shivratri drink, I can have it every day. It's the yummiest drink in the world, better than my all-time favourite strawberry milkshake. Dadi told me that it's made from a paste of soaked almonds and khus-khus (which she said is called poppy seeds in English), sugar and a little black pepper. This paste is put in a muslin cloth, which is dipped in a container of milk to give it the thandai taste. Nikhil has asked Sarla Aunty to teach him how to make thandai. He whispered to me that for the recipe, he would even endure her singing!

Maha Shivratri is a major festival, celebrated annually in honour of Lord Shiva, in the month of Magha, which corresponds to late February or March in the Gregorian calendar. Sarla Aunty told me that Maha Shivratri literally means 'the Great Night of Shiva'.

Unlike most Hindu festivals, which are celebrated during the day, Maha Shivaratri is celebrated at night and is observed with the chanting of prayers, fasting and meditating. Ardent devotees stay up the entire night, praying to Lord Shiva. People also visit Shiva temples.

Sarla Aunty did not let us leave after we had finished drinking the tasty thandai. She insisted that we have lunch with her. The lavish spread included gobi, paneer, aloo pakoras, puris, applam, pulao, boondi raita and rabri. Sarla Aunty told us that she has been fasting on Maha Shivratri since she was a teenager and chants the Shiva mantra through the day. She told us that she has learnt the tradition of jagran from her parents. She explained to us that Shivratri signifies overcoming darkness and lifting the veil of ignorance in one's life and that people must awaken or discover the Shiva inside themselves on this night.

She also told us that it is a custom to only offer intact bael leaves and not damaged or insect-eaten ones.

Interestingly, the rudraksha mala is made with the seeds of the rudraksha tree, which is said to have sprung from Lord Shiva's tears. No wonder these beads are considered holy.

Sarla Aunty explained to us that in the trinity of gods, Brahma is the creator of the universe, Vishnu the preserver and Shiva the destroyer.

I think Sarla Aunty is nice! She can't help that her singing resembles a screechy door or that she can't hold a tune. I think even Nikhil likes her a lot. In fact, he told me that he wished Dadi and *she lived on the same floor, instead of Sarla Aunty on the first floor and us on the third. Though Sarla Aunty has shoulder-length hair, her hair is so thick that she needs a big clip for her ponytail. I love her collection of clips, which always match her outfits. For Shivratri, she wore a blue clip and narrated a story to explain her choice of colour for that day.*

Lord Shiva's throat is believed to be blue because of the Halahala poison that he drank. According to legend, Shiva drank this poison when the devas and asuras or gods and demons churned the ocean for the nectar of immortality. As they churned the ocean, different types of gems, gold and silver came out of the bottom of the ocean, which were then divided equally among the gods and demons. The Halahala poison also emerged along with these other things and started to suffocate both the devas and the asuras, who then appealed to Lord Brahma and Vishnu for help. The two gods, in turn, appealed to Lord Shiva for help. Shiva drank the poison to save the world, and his body started to turn blue as the poison spread through his body. To stop the poison from spreading any further, Goddess Parvati entered Shiva's throat in the form of Mahavidya and restricted the poison there. This is the reason Shiva has a blue throat and is also called Neelkanth.

What an interesting story!

6

Being Smart on Holi

'Apply lots of coconut oil on your face and body,' Lata said. 'That way, when you play Holi, the colours won't stick to your skin or spoil it.'

'Wear your oldest clothes, which you don't mind discarding, because after you play Holi in the building, no detergent will be able to wash away the colours from your clothes. And no self-respecting washing machine will accept your clothes either!' Dadi said.

The twins emerged from the room, their faces and bodies shining with oil. They had worn their oldest pair of denim shorts and white t-shirts.

'Here are your pichkaris, or what you might know as water guns,' Lata said. 'I've filled them with coloured water.'

'It looks a bit like a pointy bicycle pump,' Nikhil said.

'You know how to use it, right?' Dadi asked.

'Of course!' The twins laughed.

'We filled these with plain water and practised with them last night; we don't want to give people an unnecessary advantage over us,' Nikhil said.

'Good,' Dadi nodded.

'Dadi, aren't you going to play Holi?' Nikhil asked.

'No,' Dadi replied. 'I'm not feeling too well.'

'Your grandmother is a scaredy-cat,' Dadu scoffed. 'She is so scared of colours that every Holi she predictably falls sick to avoid playing with colours. And thanks for teaching me the word scaredy-cat. It works perfectly for your Dadi on Holi!'

'Can *I* at least put some colour on you, Madam?' Lata asked.

'Very little, just a token amount,' Dadi relented.

Dipping her forefinger in a plate of gulal (pink powder), Lata applied a tiny dab of colour on her madam's cheek, which Dadi immediately wiped away with a paper napkin.

'Can we too apply colour on you?' the twins asked.

'Only a wee bit,' she said reluctantly.

Dipping their fingers in some coloured powder, Natasha and Nikhil dabbed a little colour on Dadi's face. Then, they dipped their hands into the powder. As they were smearing colour on Dadu's and Lata's faces, Sarla Aunty entered the house. Seeing her friend, Dadi darted into her bedroom and bolted the door from inside.

'I've never been able to catch her,' Sarla Aunty said, making a face.

The twins applied a little colour on Sarla Aunty's face.

'Oh no!' Natasha said, as Sarla Aunty patted both her

cheeks with a liberal amount of colour. Natasha ran to the mirror. She looked comical with her right cheek streaked with a dark blue powder and her left with a red one.

'Luckily, the colours will wash away fast, given the large amount of oil you two have applied on your face and body,' Sarla Aunty said.

Grabbing their pichkaris, the twins ran down the steps to play with the other children in their building complex. On the ground floor, they aimed their pichkaris and sprayed the coloured water over the other children.

'Oh no,' Natasha groaned. Someone had dropped a water balloon on her. She looked up to see Sarla Aunty holding one more balloon, which she was aiming at Nikhil's back.

Splat!

His white t-shirt was soon soaked with green colour.

'Not fair, Aunty,' he said. 'You have the advantage of aiming from the balcony.'

Aunty grinned happily. Bending down, she picked up another water balloon, which she flung at Ravi, their friend who lived on the second floor. Within a few seconds, he was soaked.

The next moment, someone flung blue powder at Natasha. Caught unawares, she looked in dismay at her white t-shirt, which now sported a big blue patch.

'You are too slow, Sis,' Nikhil laughed. Just then, one of the older children emptied a bucket of red water over Nikhil.

'You are too slow, Bro,' Natasha grinned.

Within half an hour, the twins were unrecognizable.

'Natasha, Nikhil, be careful! Don't get the colours in your eyes,' Dadi called out from the balcony.

The twins returned home an hour later, completely covered in colour.

'It's a good thing we wore our old clothes,' Natasha said.

'Yup, we just have to discard these now,' Nikhil added.

'Wait, let's click some pictures to send Mom and Dad,' Natasha said.

'Will they recognize us?' Nikhil laughed.

When they entered the dining room sometime later, after scrubbing themselves clean, they saw a platter with a strange-looking sweet on it. Nikhil picked up the semi-circular sweet. 'What is this?' he asked curiously.

'Sarla Aunty has sent this for both of you,' Dadi replied. 'It's a Sindhi sweet called pragari; she said you both will love it. The pragari has many layers of chapatis made from maida, with a khoya filling in the centre. It is deep fried till the layers become crisp.'

'It is delicious,' Nikhil said, biting into one. 'Crisp outside and filled with soft mawa inside.'

'You sound like a halwai,' Natasha said. 'But you are right, this sweet is too good. I've never eaten anything like this before in my life.'

Nikhil's Nook

Hi Friends,

I just celebrated my first Holi in India. Thanks to Lata didi (our cook-cum-housekeeper), who advised us to apply coconut oil so that the colours wouldn't stick to our skin, both Natasha and I emerged from this festival with our skins the same colour as before!

Holi, or the festival of colours, is an ancient spring festival of India, originally known as 'Holika'. Holi symbolizes the victory of good over evil and the end of winter. It is celebrated for one and a half days. It starts in the evening of the last full-moon night (Purnima) of the lunar month of Phalgun, which is February or March in the Gregorian calendar. The first evening of this festival is called Holika Dahan or Choti Holi, and the next day, which is the main day, is called Holi.

Sarla Aunty told me that the literal meaning of the word 'Holi' is 'burning'. She narrated the legend associated with Holi. A long time ago, there was a demon king called Hiranyakashyap. This demon king considered himself a god and wanted everybody in his kingdom to worship him. But to his dismay, his son Prahlad became an ardent devotee of Lord Vishnu. As Hiranyakashyap couldn't make his son worship him, he decided to get rid of him. He asked his sister Holika to enter a blazing fire with Prahlad on her lap. Holika had a boon that enabled her to enter a fire without getting burnt. Holika was unaware that the boon would work only when she entered the fire alone. She paid the price for her evil motive and burned in the fire, while Prahlad's devotion saved him. Holi celebrates the victory of good over evil and the triumph of devotion and faith. The tradition of burning Holika, or the 'Holika dahan', comes mainly from this legend.

To celebrate Holika Dahan, people gather together to perform rituals in front of the bonfire. They pray for the destruction of their inner evil and vices, the way Holika was killed in the fire. The following morning is celebrated as Rangwali Holi, when people smear each other with colours.

And before I end, I would like to mention that Sarla Aunty, my Dadi's best friend, has a great aim! She threw water balloons at us from her balcony and didn't miss a single target! And her Holi sweet was yummy. I had two. I wouldn't mind eating another!

7

Satheji's Gudi Padwa Invitation

'Who has sent this card?' Dadu held an invitation card in his hand.

'It's from Ram Sathe,' Dadi said, taking the card from him.

'We don't know any Ram Sathe,' Dadu replied.

'He is the owner of the small shop down the road,' she explained. 'Today is the opening of his new shop; he has moved into a bigger place.'

'So why has he invited us?' Dadu frowned.

'Because we are his regular customers,' Dadi replied with an irritated look on her face. 'I won't force any of you to accompany me,' she added.

The doorbell rang. Natasha ran to open the door. She didn't recognize the man who stood outside holding a box of sweets. The man had hitched his black pants over his protruding stomach and was fidgeting with the collar of his brown checked shirt. He had a small square face and the bushiest moustache Natasha had ever seen, and his eyes darted about as though they were searching for something. He coughed nervously when he saw Natasha.

'Yes?' Natasha asked.

'Satheji, come in,' Dadi said. 'What are you doing here? Shouldn't you be in your shop today for its opening?'

'My family is there, Madamji,' he said. 'I've come to give you some puran poli, Madamji, and to escort you to my shop. Without your help, I wouldn't have been able to move into a bigger place,' he said. Bending down, he touched Dadi's feet. 'You are like Annapurna for me. Bhagwan sent you to help me.'

'What are you saying, Satheji?' Dadu asked.

'Sirji, without Madamji's help, I would not even have thought of buying a bigger shop. Madamji not only helped get my daughter admitted in a college on a scholarship, she also got my son a job in her friend's husband's shop. And not just that, she also gave me money for the shop,' he said, wiping the tears from his eyes.

Everyone was surprised by his statement. They looked wide-eyed at Dadi.

'Satheji, don't worry, I'll come in some time,' she said. 'Happy Gudi Padwa to you.'

'No, Madamji, I'll wait,' he insisted. 'I wanted to open my new shop on Gudi Padwa day as it is considered auspicious, and I want you to break the coconut.'

'Satheji, you carry on, we will come on foot as I've given our driver Muniraju the day off. It's Ugadi today, which is his festival,' Dadi said.

'Okay,' Satheji replied. Looking at each of them, he joined his palms and said, 'All of you, please come.'

The entire family accompanied Dadi to Satheji's new shop. A signboard above the entrance said 'Satheji's Shop' in clear, green letters. A red ribbon, tied to the nail on the wall at either side, stretched across the doorway. Seeing the Kapoors, Satheji's family, which was gathered outside the shop, moved forward to greet them. Satheji introduced his wife, Sarita, and the three children – his son Varun, and his daughters, Radhika and Shilpa. The children took turns to touch Dadi and Dadu's feet. They even touched Lata's feet, embarrassing the housekeeper.

'Welcome, Welcome, Madamji, Sirji, Nikhilji, Natashaji and Lataji,' Satheji's voice boomed jovially. His face shone with pleasure at seeing his guests.

'I expected him to call us childrenji,' Nikhil whispered.

Natasha tried to keep a straight face.

Dadi handed Satheji a gift-wrapped box.

'No, no, Madamji, you have done enough,' he said. 'I can't accept this gift.'

'This is for good luck,' she replied. 'Don't you want to move into a bigger shop?'

'Of course, Madamji.' He flushed with pleasure. 'Thank

you,' he said, accepting the colourfully wrapped gift. Passing the packet to his daughter, Radhika, who stood close by dressed in a green sari, he took the coconut from his wife and handed it to Dadi.

Dadi broke the coconut in the first attempt. Everyone clapped. Next, Satheji offered a pair of scissors to Dadi. After Dadi had cut the ribbon, Satheji's wife performed aarti for the entire Kapoor family and showered them with flower petals.

'Wait, a photo with all of you,' Satheji said, as everyone began to stroll into the shop. Varun quickly brought out a camera. The group stood stiffly as Varun clicked a few photographs. Handing the camera to a customer who had ambled into the shop, Varun joined the group for the last photograph.

'I feel so important,' Nikhil said.

'So do I,' Lata whispered. 'Now I know how film stars and VIPs must feel.'

Dadi bought a box of chocolates and a few packets of biscuits and chips. When she handed Satheji the money, he insisted that he couldn't accept any payment from her.

'It's boni, Satheji,' she said. 'Keep it in your cashbox; it will bring you luck.'

They all walked back home, munching on the chips from the packet Lata had opened.

'I had no idea my wife was so philanthropic,' Dadu put his arm around Dadi. 'Now I know what happened to the prize money.'

'We are proud of you, Dadi,' Nikhil said.

Natasha asked, 'What's boni, Dadi? We heard you say that word to Satheji.'

'Boni is the first earning of the day and is considered auspicious by shopkeepers,' Dadi replied.

Natasha's Journal

Dadi has become my inspiration. I want to be just like her when I grow up. Her behaviour towards everybody is so full of warmth. No wonder everyone loves her.

Satheji inaugurated his new shop on Gudi Padwa, which is a popular festival celebrated in Maharashtra. Gudi Padwa, or New Year, is considered auspicious for starting new ventures. It signifies the reaping of the rabi crop and signals the arrival of spring.

It is celebrated on the first day of the month of Chaitra, which is calculated according to the lunisolar Hindu calendar. Chaitra typically falls in March or April of the Gregorian calendar. I was so happy that Satheji asked Dadi to inaugurate his shop. It was a nice gesture. I sent Mom and Dad the photos I had clicked of Dadi breaking the coconut and cutting the ribbon. They immediately called Dadi to congratulate her. Dad teased her saying he was now the son of a celebrity and asked her if she would be able to spare some time for him when he came to India.

When I complimented Satheji's daughter on the beautiful rangoli she had made outside her father's shop, she offered to teach me how to make it. Dadi said we could either make it in the corner of the puja room or in the balcony. Radhika explained to me that it was considered auspicious to decorate your home with flowers and rangoli on Gudi Padwa. She told me that processions and community parades called Shobha Yatras were taken out on this day.

She also showed me the unique Gudi flag, which is made by tying a yellow, red or green silk cloth with a zari border to the tip of a bamboo stick and inverting a copper or silver kalash (pot) over it. This is then covered with garlands of marigold and decorated with mango and neem leaves. The Gudi flag is believed to ward off evil and bring prosperity and good luck into the house. The inverted copper vessel signifies victory and achievement.

She further added that the Gudi symbolizes Lord Rama's victory over Ravana, and the Gudi Padwa festival celebrates Lord Rama's coronation as the King of Ayodhya after he completed fourteen years in exile.

We ate the puris and shrikhand Satheji's wife had made. The puran poli was delicious. I had two. But Nikhil beat me, as usual, by having three! Puran poli is a traditional Maharashtrian sweet. Radhika promised to teach me how to make puran poli too. I think Nikhil's passion for cooking is rubbing off on me!

8

Good News on Ugadi

When Nikhil and Natasha reached home, their driver, Muniraju was waiting outside the flat with his wife and children. His son and daughter were chasing each other in the corridor. Seeing them, the children ran back and stood quietly behind their parents.

'The watchman told me that you all had gone to Satheji's shop, so I decided to wait,' Muniraju said.

'I couldn't recognize you!' Natasha exclaimed, as she had never seen the driver in anything other than his white uniform. Muniraju was wearing a pale-yellow shirt over a cream dhoti. He had a square face and long wiry hair, which was tucked behind his ears.

'It's Ugadi, so I'm wearing my traditional clothes,' he said. 'Please meet Shashikala,' he added, introducing his wife to Dadi and Dadu.

The woman in the red sari was short, with neatly plaited long hair. A string of jasmine flowers was draped around her plait, like a snake coiled around a tree. Her light skin flushed as she smiled shyly, revealing symmetrical teeth. Bending down, she touched Dadi and Dadu's feet. 'No, no,' Dadu said. 'Please don't touch my feet.'

'Sir, you two are like our parents. We need your blessings. My children, Vanitha and Raja – you saw them when they were very young,' he said, gesturing towards his son and daughter. 'Vanitha is four years old and Raja will be six in a few months,' he added proudly.

Both the children were thin with small faces and eyes that were large and set wide apart. They also had their father's curly hair and mother's light skin.

The two children moved to the front and bowed to touch the feet of the elders there. Once again, Lata flushed at this unexpected respect. Before the twins could react, Vanitha and Raja touched their feet too.

'They must have been told at home to touch the feet of people even a few years older than them,' Nikhil muttered.

Removing a bunch of keys from her handbag, Lata opened the door, and they all trooped into the house.

'Happy Ugadi to all of you,' Dadi wished them. 'Please sit down.'

Muniraju and his family squatted on the ground.

'No, no, please sit on the sofa,' Dadi said. The four of them sat awkwardly on a large sofa. The children sat on their parents' laps. 'Muniraju, I asked you to take a holiday today. Why did you come?'

'To give you our good news,' he said. 'And to take yours and sir's blessings, Madam,' he said. 'As both our parents live in the village, my wife came to seek your blessings before starting her work tomorrow. She has got a job in a playschool as a helper.'

'That's wonderful, Muniraju,' Dadi smiled.

'Your idea worked, Madam,' Muniraju said. 'You asked me to enroll Shashikala for English-speaking classes with Sarla Madam's niece, which helped her get the job. And thanks to you and Sarla Madam for paying the money. After we take your blessings, we will visit Sarla Madam too.'

'Sarla Madam's niece is a very good teacher,' Shashikala said, then asked, 'Madam, you remember this sari?'

Dadi knit her brows, trying to remember.

'You sent it for Diwali last year,' Shashikala said. 'I saved it for Ugadi. I love this colour!'

'The colour suits you,' Dadi smiled warmly. 'I'm happy you liked it.'

'Lata, bring some chocolates for the children,' Dadi instructed.

The housekeeper brought a tray filled with chocolates, barfis and pedas.

Seeing Vanitha and Raja turn to their parents as though asking for permission to eat the sweets, Dadi said, 'Take as many as you want.'

Vanitha and Raja promptly picked up a peda each.

'Madam, you all must have this,' Shashikala said, taking out a steel box from her wicker basket. It contained pieces of jaggery, small white flowers and green leaves. 'It's bevu bella. It's a tradition to have this on Ugadi,' she said, offering the container to Dadi.

After Dadi, Dadu and Lata each picked up a small piece of jaggery and a leaf and put it in their mouth, Natasha too reached out for one. She scooped up a piece of jaggery, a leaf and a few flowers and placed them on her tongue. The sweetness of the jaggery balanced out the bitter taste of the white flowers and the leaf. Even before she could figure out the taste or warn her brother, Nikhil had scooped up a good amount and shoved it in his mouth. Sadly, his portion had more flowers and leaves than jaggery. As everyone watched, Nikhil's expression quickly changed to one of dismay. Tears rolled down his cheeks as the bitterness of the neem leaves and the flowers hit his palate.

'You should have eaten a small portion of it,' Dadi said, handing him the plate of pedas. 'Have a sweet, it will remove the bitter taste in your mouth.'

'Bevu bella is made by mixing jaggery, which is prepared from the fresh harvest of sugarcane, and the leaves of the neem tree,' Shashikala said. 'And I've also brought the Ugadi pachadi. This is a custom I've picked up from Andhra Pradesh as my family lived there for several years.'

'I'll be careful before eating anything else brought by

her,' Nikhil whispered to his sister.

'Haven't you learnt anything from Master Chef?' Natasha said. 'You should always taste a little bit first, and only if you like the dish should you take a generous helping. I always knew your gluttony would get you into trouble one day.'

Her brother scowled.

Shashikala pulled out a garland of mango leaves that had been strung together on a coarse white thread from her basket. 'Madam, it's customary to tie this over the door. I made one for our house and one for yours.'

'That's so sweet of you,' Dadi smiled. 'Muniraju, please hang it over our door.'

Nikhil's Nook

Hi Friends,

I'm back with another festival.

Ugadi, also spelled as Yugadi, is the New Year for the people of Karnataka, Andhra Pradesh and Telangana. It is celebrated on the first day of the Hindu month of Chaitra, which coincides with March or April of the Gregorian calendar. Ugadi comes from the Sanskrit word 'yug', which means age or era, and 'adi', which means beginning. So, it literally means the beginning of a new era or the beginning of a new age. Ugadi, also known as Chaitra Suddha Padhyami, is believed to be the day when Lord Brahma created the universe.

On Ugadi, people draw colourful rangolis outside their houses. They decorate their doorways with strings of mango leaves. As on other festivals, they buy new clothes and wear them on Ugadi day after an oil bath. One of the traditions of Ugadi, which people of Andhra Pradesh follow, is to make a special dish called Ugadi Pachadi. This dish combines different flavours—sweet, sour, salty and bitter—and is made from tamarind paste, neem leaves, brown sugar or sweet jaggery, salt, pepper and pieces of green mango. Interestingly, the variety of flavours are symbolic of the bittersweet experiences that come one's way in life. Bevu bella, another traditional Ugadi dish, is also symbolic of the same thing. A mix of sweet and bitter, it is prepared from freshly harvested sugarcane and the flower buds and leaves of the neem tree. This mixture is eaten after the pre-lunch puja. Believe me, the neem leaves are lethal! The bitterness made my taste buds go into shock. So, be careful if you are offered Bevu bella or pachadi.

Muniraju told me that on Ugadi, people worship the panchang (almanac) to have a prosperous new year ahead.

I wish Natasha had warned me about the neem leaves. My tongue still feels bitter. She got her revenge for the day I had garlanded the cow and left the buffalo for her.

To compensate for the bitterness in my mouth, I had to eat two pedas and one barfi!

9

Sarla Aunty's
Cheti Chand Treat

Ever since Sarla Aunty had sent special homemade treats for Nikhil, they had hit it off well. And after sampling her pragari—the traditional Sindhi sweet made on Holi—he could not stop praising her. He had conveniently forgotten that her singing voice was like a hundred screeching doors.

'What a turncoat you are!' Natasha said.

'I never said anything against Sarla Aunty, it was just her offkey singing that I had commented on,' Nikhil defended himself. 'I've always found her to be a sweet lady, and I became a fan after I realized that, like Dadi, she too has a heart as soft as cotton candy, or should one say softer than the yummy gulab jamuns she makes!'

'Fan of hers or her cooking?' Natasha raised her eyebrows.

'First a fan of Sarla Aunty, then her cooking,' Nikhil said. 'Her aloo tuks are to die for,' he sighed. 'She has promised to teach me how to make them.'

'Next time she sends the aloo tuks, I'll take the larger share,' Natasha said.

'But she sends them for me,' Nikhil said, arching his eyebrows.

'Stop arguing, children.' Dadi entered the room carrying a plate of aloo tuks.

Aloo tuks are potatoes cut in halves and deep fried twice (they are flattened after they are fried the first time) and sprinkled with pepper and chaat masala before being served.

'Sarla sent them for both of you. Today's lunch is being sent by Sarla as it's Cheti Chand, the Sindhi new year. In fact, she wanted to invite us home for lunch, but she had to leave for her sister-in-law's house. She will be back by teatime and has invited us for tea, instead.'

'Cool,' Nikhil said, grabbing two aloo tuks, 'she is the best cook in the world.' But seeing Dadi's expression, he quickly added, 'I mean the best cook after you.'

'Sarla has a heart of gold,' Dadi said, putting an aloo tuk into her mouth. 'I've never been able to make these properly. I've tried a few times, but these pesky aloo tuks always turn out too soft. But that's okay, since Sarla sends them whenever she makes kadhi-chawal.'

'Her Sindhi kadhi is delicious,' Natasha said. 'Sarla Aunty is as good a cook as you.'

'And she is generous too.' Nikhil was eating his fourth tuk.

'Save some for Dadu. He also loves these tuks, as does Lata,' Natasha said.

'I've kept some aside for them' Dadi smiled. 'I had to save them from my young glutton here!'

'Do you want me to serve you lunch now, or would you like to wait for Dadu?'

'We will wait,' Nikhil said, taking his fifth tuk.

Just then, the doorbell rang.

'Looks like your Dadu has returned.'

Five minutes later, Lata summoned them for lunch. The table was groaning with Sindhi delicacies: tomato kadhi, white rice, sai bhaji, tairi, dahi vadas and sweet boondi.

'It all looks so yummy,' Nikhil said.

'It must be Cheti Chand. Neither you nor Lata can make kadhi as good as this,' Dadu said, taking a generous helping. 'And why has she sent so few aloo tuks?' he asked.

'She had sent loads, but Nikhil has already attacked them,' Natasha said, grinning. 'Dadu, you now have a food-gobbling monster in your house.'

'Our house, Natasha,' Dadi said

gently. 'Now it's yours and Nikhil's too.'

'Yes,' Dadu nodded. Then, with a mock-serious expression, he added, 'Looks like I'll have to buy more ration from now on.'

They all laughed.

'Dadi, what do Sindhis do on Cheti Chand?' Natasha asked curiously.

'Sarla will be the best person to explain that to you,' Dadi replied with a smile.

'Isn't this tairi a little bit like sweet pongal?' Nikhil asked. He had licked his bowl of tairi clean and was now eyeing the sweet boondi.

'How are your studies?' Dadu asked.

'Lata's nephew, who is studying engineering, is helping them with Science and Maths. And Sarla's niece, who conducts coaching classes, is polishing their Hindi,' Dadi said.

'That's good,' Dadu smiled. 'I was a bit concerned.'

'Too late to show your concern!' Dadi made a face. 'I arranged for their coaching classes way back in January and it is mid-March now! They have their exams in the first week of April!'

Natasha's Journal

We had the best high tea of our lives at Sarla Aunty's house. She had made Sindhi dal pakwan — pakwan, or teekra as it is called in Sindhi, is made from maida. Like Nikhil, I too have become extremely fond of Sarla Aunty. Sushil Uncle is sweet too, though he is hardly at home. Both their daughters are married — one is settled in London and the other in Hong Kong.

Sarla Aunty explained to us that Cheti Chand is the Sindhi New Year. She said that this festival typically falls in late March or early April in the Gregorian Calendar, around the same time as Gudi Padwa in Maharashtra and Ugadi in South India.

The festival of Cheti Chand signifies the arrival of spring and the harvest season. It celebrates the birth of Jhulelal (also known as Uderolal or Odero Lal). According to legend, in the year 1007, the people of the Sindh region prayed to the Hindu God Varuna, on the banks of the Indus River, to save them from the cruelty of a tyrannical ruler called Mirkhshah. This Muslim ruler was from Thatta, the medieval capital of Sindh.

Sarla Aunty said that a vision of Varuna is believed to have appeared and assured the people that he would be born as an infant in Nasirpur so that he could save them. The baby was born on the first day of the Hindu month of Chaitra, which, in the Sindhi language, is called Chet. He was called Jhulelal. When Mirkhshah heard about the baby's birth, he sent his minister to kill the infant with a poisoned rose petal. However, when the minister saw Jhulelal, the baby smiled at him and the poisoned rose petal fell from his hand. A moment later, when the minister looked at Jhulelal again, the baby had turned into an old man. And within a second, he became a young man and then transformed into a warrior on horseback. The minister rushed back to tell Mirkshah about these strange happenings. Mirkshah, in turn, asked that Jhulelal be brought to the banks of the Indus River so that he could see the mysterious man. Jhulelal appeared on the banks of the river as a warrior on horseback, along with a large army. Seeing the large army, the minister got scared. When the minister beseeched him to control his army, Jhulelal suddenly disappeared. All of this made Mirkshah so angry that he ordered that all Hindus should convert to Islam immediately.

Fearing the worst, the Hindus panicked and went to Jhulelal's house in Nasirpur. The infant Jhulelal calmly assured them of his protection and asked them to assemble at a temple near the Indus River. When the Hindus assembled on the banks of the river, a firestorm engulfed Mirkshah's palace. Mirkshah managed to escape the raging fire with great difficulty and reached the temple where Jhulelal stood in his warrior avatar. He realized that Jhulelal was not an ordinary person and fell at his feet, begging forgiveness. Jhulelal immediately dismissed the storm. It is further believed that Jhulelal turned into an old man and impressed upon Mirkshah that both Muslims and Hindus need to be given the freedom to practise their faiths.

Following this, Jhulelal championed the cause of religious freedom in Sindh. Owing to this legend, Sindhis celebrate the new year as

Jhulelal or Uderolal's birthday.

The word 'Sindhi' is derived from the Sindhu River (now the Indus River in Pakistan). When Sindhi men went out to sea, their women prayed to Jhulelal for their safe return by offering a prasad called akha. Akha is made from rice, sugar, a cardamom, a clove and a white flower. Some Sindhis greet each other with the words Jai Jhulelal or Jhulelal Bera Paar.

Sarla Aunty said that on this day, many Sindhis take barana to lakes and rivers. Barana consists of crystallized sugar or misri, cardamom, fruit, flowers, a diya filled with oil and a kalash. The kalash is a small copper vessel filled with water. A coconut is placed on this kalash and covered with a red cloth and flowers. She said that some people also carry a statue of Jhulelal along with the kalash.

By the time Sarla Aunty had narrated the story of Cheti Chand, I was eating my third pakwan. I gulped when I realized that I had eaten just one pakwan less than Nikhil had! Granted they were the size of puris, but if I didn't watch out, I would soon become a glutton like my brother.

10

A Gift on Ram Navami

The older Kapoors had gone to their friend's house for breakfast, leaving strict instructions with Lata that by no means were the twins to watch television. Nikhil and Natasha were studying for their exams in Nikhil's room. Every now and then, Lata would enter the room on one pretext or the other.

On her fifth visit into the room, Nikhil closed his textbook in exasperation and stared at the housekeeper. 'You can see that I'm really studying. I haven't sneaked any novel into the middle of my textbook.' Holding his textbook by its spine, he waved it in the air.

'I just came to ask if you were hungry,' Lata said quickly.

'You asked that three times before,' Natasha scowled. 'I'm sure Dadi asked you to check up on us, and you are doing a poor job of it.'

'We have been studying non-stop since early morning,' Nikhil said. 'We just took a twenty-minute break for breakfast.'

'You have been good,' Lata said. 'We are just concerned that as you aren't used to the Indian school syllabus, your grades could go down.'

'Lata didi, can we take a half-hour break?' Natasha asked. 'We will just go down and meet Sarla Aunty. We haven't seen her in days.'

'Okay,' she said. 'Just thirty minutes. And when did you become a fan of Sarla Madam's? I know that she is Nikhil's favourite aunt.'

'I've always liked her,' Natasha said.

Closing their textbooks, the twins walked out of the room. Then they raced down the stairs, forgetting to close the main door behind them.

When Nikhil rang the Sadhwanis' doorbell, their housekeeper, Bela, opened the door almost immediately, as though she had been waiting for them.

'Lata called me on the intercom and told me you two were coming,' she smiled. 'She asked me to send you back within half an hour.'

'Lata didi is worse than a school principal,' Nikhil muttered. 'Is Sarla Aunty at home?'

'Yes, she is in the puja room,' Bela said.

Removing their slippers in the living room, the twins walked into the puja room. Sarla Aunty sat cross-legged on the blue mat. In her lap was a thick book. The twins sat on either side of her. The book she was reading was voluminous. It also looked old, its pages having yellowed with time.

Though Sarla Aunty had noticed them come in, she didn't take her eyes off the book. Natasha stared at the idols of the gods and goddesses in Sarla Aunty's puja room. It was like a panorama of the gods of the Hindu pantheon. In the centre stood a tall idol of Krishna with a flute to his lips. To his left sat a brass idol of Ganesha and to the right a marble one of goddess Lakshmi, both draped in silk. Shiva stood close by, in a posture that Sarla Aunty called the Nataraj posture, with a leopard print cloth on his waist and a rudraksha bead necklace around his neck. Sarla Aunty was fond of making clothes for the gods and goddesses, or vagas as she referred to them in Sindhi.

After some time, Sarla Aunty closed the large, impressive-looking book and began to wrap it in a velvet cloth. The twins tried to quickly read the title on the plain brown cover. 'Ramayana', it said in large letters.

'Ah, you two are just in time to have the Ram Navami prasad,' Sarla Aunty said as she removed the cover from a steel dish and placed two large yellow pedas in the twins' palms.

'Why were you reading the Ramayana?' Nikhil asked, taking a big bite of the peda.

'I read it twice a year. I try to finish my first reading on Ram Navami and then the second on

Dussehra,' she smiled.

'How long does it take you to read it, Aunty?' Natasha asked.

'Depends on how many pages I read in a day,' she said. 'Before I forget, I have a gift for the two of you.' She lifted two books from a pile of five that lay on a wooden stand to the side.

'Here you go,' she said, handing a copy each to Nikhil and Natasha. 'Ramayana in English for Young Readers' was written clearly on the cover of each book.

'Wow!' Natasha said, hugging Sarla Aunty.

'It's in simple English, so you both can understand it easily,' she said. 'I bought copies for Mr Rao's grandchildren, Raunak and Reema, too. The Ramayana is a complex and wonderful epic. You can start by reading a page or two

every day and slowly immerse yourself in it to understand its meaning.'

The twins nodded.

'How are your studies?' she asked. 'Have you finished revising your syllabus?'

'Yes, Aunty,' Nikhil said. 'We have been studying hard. We don't want to disappoint Dadu and Dadi.'

'I wanted to visit you all, but I thought my visit would distract you both,' she said. 'Now go back home and study, and after your exams are over, come and spend the day with me. I'll make your favourite aloo tuk, Nikhil.' And then, turning to Natasha, she added, 'And your favourite Sindhi kadhi.'

'Cool!' Nikhil said. 'Please make lots of aloo tuks, Aunty, because my appetite always increases after the exams are over. I think the post-exam stress makes me hungry!' He made a face.

They all laughed.

Nikhil's Nook

Hi Friends,

I received a wonderful gift today from Sarla Aunty. A copy of the epic Ramayana.

I think the Ramayana is going to be a very interesting book. I am looking forward to reading it after my exams. The story of Lord Rama seems quite fascinating. His birthday is celebrated on Ram Navami. Sarla Aunty said that this Hindu or Vedic festival is part of the spring Navratri. Rama was born on the ninth day of the lunar month of Chaitra. The Ram Navami festival occurs in the Gregorian months of March or April every year, when we have our final exams.

Rama, also known as Ramachandra, was the seventh avatar of Lord Vishnu. Sarla Aunty explained that according to the ancient Hindu scriptures, Lord Vishnu, the preserver of the universe, comes in various incarnations or avatars to show the world the path of righteousness. In the Hindu trinity, Vishnu is the preserver, Brahma the creator, and Shiva the protector or destroyer of all evil.

Rama was the eldest son of Dasharath, the king of Ayodhya. Dasharath had three wives: Kaushalya, Kaikeyi and Sumitra. Lord Rama was Dasharath's son from his eldest wife, Kaushalya. His brothers Lakshman and Shatrughan were born to Dasharath's middle wife, Sumitra, and Bharat, the youngest, to his youngest wife, Kaikeyi. Lord Rama won Sita's hand in a Swayamvar organized by Sita's father, King Janaka of Mithila.

The *Swayamvar was an archery contest. I think an archery contest sounds so exciting! As the story goes, one day, Bharat's mother, Kaikeyi, reminded Dasharath of his promise of granting her a wish. Kaikeyi wanted Bharat to become the king, so she demanded that Rama be exiled from the kingdom for fourteen years. Dasharath was grief-stricken, but Rama did not want his father to break his promise and left for the forest with Sita and Lakshman. Rama wandered in the forest for ten years before arriving in Panchvati on the banks of the Godavari River. Panchvati was also the abode of the rakshashas. One day, a demoness called Shurpanakha saw Rama and wanted to entice him. When Rama refused, she approached Lakshman. When Lakshman refused her too, she threatened to harm Sita. Hearing this, Lakshman cut off her nose. When her brother, Ravana, the King of Lanka, heard of this, he decided to take revenge. He arrived in Panchvati and kidnapped Sita. On finding Sita missing, Rama and Lakshman travelled south and met Sugriva, the ruler of the Vanar kingdom of Kishikindha. They also met his advisor, Hanuman. Then, along with an army of monkeys, they made a bridge to Lanka and crossed over to rescue Sita. Ravana was defeated in the ensuing war. Rama rescued Sita and returned to Ayodhya along with Lakshman. Rama was crowned king on his return.*

Ram Navami is celebrated in various ways. Besides readings of the Ramayana, some people also adorn a statue of the infant Rama with silk clothes and flowers, the way Sarla Aunty had done, and place it in a cradle. Although the day is primarily dedicated to Rama, Lakshman, Sita and Hanuman are also worshipped as they played an important role in Rama's life. Temples also organize charitable events and community meals.

Sarla Aunty has a lovely painting of Lord Rama in the forest, holding a bow and arrow. The gentle expression on Lord Rama's face is very endearing.

And the malai pedas were yummy!

11

Dadi's Maun Vrat on Mahavir Jayanti

Dadu had driven the car to school to pick up Nikhil and Natasha, as Muniraju had taken the day off to take his daughter to the dentist. The twins' preliminary exams, or prelims as they are more popularly called, had started. Goodwin Convent School had an unusual system of holding the preliminary exams a few days before the final exams as they believed that this helped prepare their students for the stress of exams.

As soon as the children got into the back seat of the car, their grandmother turned around to study their faces. Their expressions usually gave away how they had fared in the exam. But today, both their faces were expressionless.

'How was the paper?' Dadi asked.

'Not bad,' Nikhil said.

'Good,' Natasha replied.

Both Dadi and Dadu laughed gently at their brief replies.

Dadu had been carefully navigating the heavy traffic, but when they stopped at a traffic signal, he turned around and winked at them. 'I love the way you two confuse your grandmother,' he said.

Dadi unwrapped a foil paper and handed them each a cheese sandwich, saying, 'The heavy traffic will delay our lunch.'

Soon, the signal light changed and they were on their way again. Natasha looked out from the window. Two monks in white clothes were walking barefoot on the road. They both held small brooms with which they were sweeping the road ahead of them as they walked. Both had covered their heads with a cloth. As Natasha pressed her face to the window, her nose left a tiny smudge on the glass.

She squinted, trying to see their faces.

'Why are those people in white sweeping the ground?' she asked.

'They are Jain monks,' Dadi said. 'They sweep the ground before them as they walk, so that they don't accidentally step on tiny insects.'

'Why do they wear that cloth over their mouth?' Nikhil asked.

'Jain monks cover their mouths with cloth so that they don't harm the tiny organisms, which often get killed while speaking,' Dadi explained. 'These monks believe in Ahimsa or non-violence.'

'You believe in all religions. You even follow the customs of a few of them. But, sadly, you don't follow one aspect of Jainism,' Dadu teased.

'And which one is that?' his wife asked.

'Maun Vrat or vow of silence,' he said, trying to keep a straight face. 'The Jains follow Maun Ekadashi, which you, Sarla and Lata, should follow at least once every few days. In fact, if you can keep quiet even for an hour, I'll never tease the three of you again.'

Dadi sat stiffly in her seat. Keeping her index finger over her lips, she turned her face away and looked out of the window.

'Do you want me to pick up idlis for lunch?' Dadu asked.
Dadi shook her head.

'What is for lunch?' Nikhil asked.

Dadi didn't reply. Instead, she started typing something on her mobile phone. The twins exchanged puzzled looks while Dadu frowned at his wife.

'Nikhil asked you something,' he said.

Turning around, Dadi lifted her mobile phone. She had typed, 'fried rice, butter paneer, chapatis and bread pudding'.

'Yummy,' Nikhil said.

'Do you have a sore throat, Dadi?' Natasha asked.

Once again, Dadi started typing. She showed her phone to the twins. She had typed, 'I'm on Maun Vrat'.

'Maun Vrat?' Nikhil looked alarmed. 'I have my Hindi prelim exam tomorrow. Who will teach me if you take a vow of silence?'

Nikhil's face fell as Dadi started typing again. But when he saw what she had typed, he grinned.

'My Maun Vrat will be over in 45 minutes.'

'Cool,' he sighed. 'We will reach home by then.'

'Today is Mahavir Jayanti,' Dadu said. 'The monks must be on their way to the Jain temple nearby.'

The two Jain monks turned into a lane on the right and soon disappeared from view.

As they drove over a flyover, Dadi turned around and showed the twins her phone. 'Tell your Dadu he forgot to pick up his suit from the dry cleaners.'

'Dadu, you forgot to pick up your suit from the dry cleaners,' Nikhil said.

'Oh no,' Dadu groaned. 'Couldn't you have reminded me?' he stared accusingly at his wife.

Dadi held up her phone. 'Maun Vrat' was written on it.

'Now I can't even turn back as we are on the flyover,' Dadu grumbled. 'I needed the suit for the party at the Army Club this evening. I will have to go back to the laundry after dropping you all home.'

Dadi showed the twins her phone. She had typed, 'Now you know why I don't go on a Maun Vrat.'

The twins exchanged looks.

Then, with a smile on her face, Dadi switched on the car stereo. The lyrics of a popular song filled the car.

Dadu scowled at the wheel!

Natasha's Journal

I was very curious to know more about Mahavir Jayanti as I was fascinated by the two monks with the serene look on their faces.

Once Dadi had ended her Maun Vrat, I asked her to tell me about Mahavir Jayanti in detail. Dadi told me that Mahavir Jayanti is also known as Mahavir Janma Kalyanak and is one of most important Jain festivals. It usually occurs in the month of March or April of the Gregorian calendar.

The day celebrates the birth of Lord Mahavir, the twenty-fourth and last Tirthankara (spiritual teacher) of the Jains. Lord Mahavir, also known as Vardhamana Mahavira, was born in Kshatriyakund, Vaishali (the ancient name for Bihar) to King Siddhartha and Queen Trishala in the early part of the 6th century BCE. Mahavir is believed to have abandoned worldly possessions at the age of thirty. He left his family to become an ascetic. Mahavir meditated for the next twelve to thirteen years, at the end of which he attained Kevala Jnana or Omniscience. In Jainism, a Tirthankara is an individual who has conquered the samsara, or the cycle of birth and death. According to Jain philosophy, Tirthankaras are human beings who attained enlightenment through meditation and self-realization.

Interestingly, twenty-two of the twenty-four Tirthankars of Jainism, including Mahavir, were born in the Ikshvaku dynasty. Even Gautama Buddha is believed to have been born during this dynasty.

Dadi outlined the five principles of Jainism. Ahimsa or non-violence is the first, truth or satya the second, non-stealing or achaurya the third, chastity or brahmacharya the fourth and non-attachment (non-possession) or aparigraha the fifth.

I'm completely enchanted by the serene expression on Lord Mahavir's face. I've decided that in my holidays, I'll read more about Mahavir and the Ikshvaku dynasty.

Poor Dadu had to drive back later to pick up his suit from the dry cleaners. I wish he hadn't challenged Dadi about the maun vrat!

12

A Secret Revealed
on Hanuman Jayanti

'Nikhil, Natasha, could you please go to the Sadhwanis' flat and get me the file with the building repair quotations from Sushil?' Dadi said.

'I'll go, Dadi,' Natasha said. 'I wanted a break from studying anyway.'

'Just make sure that your break is not longer than your study period,' Dadi said worriedly.

'Stop stressing, Dadi,' Natasha said, making a face. 'I've revised most of the syllabus.' Then, she asked, 'Dadi, why aren't both you and Dadu in the building committee?'

'Is your grandfather ever at home?' Dadi raised her eyebrows. 'He is always busy playing snooker and golf. He has no time for anything else in life!'

Natasha skipped out of the house.

'Come back fast,' Dadi called out behind her.

Natasha always looked forward to spending time with

Sarla Aunty and Sushil Uncle. They were the same age as her grandparents. Like Sarla Aunty, Sushil Uncle was also an excellent storyteller.

Bela opened the Sadhwanis' door the moment Natasha reached the first-floor landing.

Natasha wasn't surprised. Her Dadi must obviously have called on the intercom to announce her arrival!

The house resonated with Sushil Uncle's clear voice reciting a prayer.

'Good morning, Natasha,' Sarla Aunty said as she emerged from the kitchen, wiping her hands with a towel.

'Good morning, Aunty,' Natasha said. 'What prayer is uncle reciting?'

'It's the Hanuman Chalisa – a prayer recited to invoke Lord Hanuman,' she replied. 'Your uncle has been reciting it for fifty-five years now! He started when he was only seven.'

'Wow, that is a very long time,' Natasha said.

A short while later, Sushil Uncle emerged from the puja room. He was tall with fair skin and a square, flushed face that always looked as though he had just run a marathon. His eyebrows looked like two millipedes ready to do a headbutt.

'Good morning,' he said.

'Good morning, Uncle. Dadi wants the quotation file for the building repair work,' Natasha said.

'Yes, she spoke to me about it last night,' he nodded.

'Uncle, why do you recite the Hanuman Chalisa every day?' Natasha asked. 'Aunty said you have been reciting this prayer for the last fifty-five years.'

'Sit down,' Sushil Uncle led her to the sofa. 'I'll tell you a story. Today is Hanuman Jayanti, so I feel like sharing a few secrets with you.'

Both Sarla Aunty and Natasha made themselves comfortable on the sofa beside him. Natasha noticed that Bela didi, too, had abandoned her work in the kitchen and was trying to listen in.

'When I was around seven years old, my grandmother narrated stories about Hanuman's bravery. According to one story, Rahu—a Vedic planet—was pursuing the Sun for a scheduled eclipse, Hanuman too was chasing the sun at the same time. It is said that Hanuman thrashed Rahu so that he could reach the Sun first.

Another legend talks of how Hanuman carried the entire Dronagiri mountain in the Himalayas when Lord Rama asked him to fetch the healing Sanjeevani herb that grew on it. The herb was needed to cure Lakshman after he was injured in the battle against Ravana. Hanuman carried the entire mountain to Lord Rama,' Sushil Uncle added.

'Then?' Natasha prodded, curious to hear more.

'As a young boy, I was scared of sleeping alone in my room at night,' he continued. 'My grandmother gave me a picture of Hanuman and asked me to place it on my dresser, saying that I should try to think of Hanuman as my protector. Interestingly, after I placed his picture in my room, I stopped being scared of the dark. Hanuman became my superhero. I wanted to become like him, brave and powerful, full of energy and strength. My grandmother also gave me the Hanuman Chalisa. I started reciting it every day, hoping to get Hanuman's strength to fly and lift mountains,' he said, smiling. 'I even tried to jump from my bed with my hands stretched out to fly like he did, but instead, I fell and grazed my knees!' he added sheepishly.

Natasha and Sarla Aunty laughed. And so did Sushil Uncle!

'When I told my grandmother how I had hurt my knees, she laughed and said, "Hanuman is a god, which is why he could do these acts of bravery. Rather than trying to be powerful like him, you can imbibe his other qualities, such as devotion and humility."'

The doorbell rang.

When Bela opened the door, Nikhil stood outside.

'I didn't want to miss out on the fun,' he said, entering the house.

Sushil Uncle repeated a few stories of Hanuman for Nikhil.

Nikhil's Nook

Hi Friends,
  I'm fascinated by the story of Hanuman.
  According to legend, Lord Hanuman was born on the Anjaneri

mountain to an apsara called Anjana. It is believed that Anjana had been born on Earth due to a curse and was redeemed from this curse when her son was born. The Valmiki Ramayana states that his father, Kesari, was the son of King Brihaspati of Sumeru. Kesari and Anjana had prayed for a child to Shiva for twelve years before Hanuman was born. Hanuman is also considered an incarnation of Shiva. Some believe him to be the son of the wind god, Vayu (in many verses, he is called Vayuputra), as Vayu is said to have played a role in his birth. And he is also known as Bajrang Bali, as it is said that he had limbs as hard as vajra or bajra. In Sanskrit, both Bajrang and Vajrang mean diamond, and bali is symbolic of Hanuman's divine strength.

Sushil Uncle narrated another story about the birth of Hanuman. Once, Narada became infatuated with a princess, so he went to Lord Vishnu to ask him to make him look grand and handsome like a god – to give him a Hari Mukh (Hari is another name for Vishnu and Mukh means face), so that the princess would garland him at her swayamvara. Vishnu gave him the face of a vanara (monkey) instead. Narada was completely unaware, and when he went for the swayamvara with the face of a monkey, the entire court, including the princess, laughed at him.

Narada was unable to bear this humiliation and went to Vishnu's abode and cursed him, saying that since he had given Narada the face of a monkey, one day, he would be dependent on a vanara. Vishnu tried to pacify Narada, telling him that it was for Narada's own good as his powers would decrease were he to marry. On hearing this, Narada was filled with remorse. But Vishnu comforted him saying that the curse would turn into a boon, for it would lead to the birth of Hanuman, an avatar of Shiva. And Vishnu's avatar, Rama, could not have killed Ravana without the help of Hanuman, a vanara. Hanuman was extremely devoted to Rama.

Hanuman Janam-utsav or Hanuman Jayanti celebrates the birth of Lord Hanuman. This festival is celebrated on different days in different parts of India. In most states of India, the festival falls either in March or in April of the Gregorian calendar.

On Hanuman Jayanti, people visit Hanuman temples, sing devotional songs in honour of Hanuman and chant prayers like the Hanuman Chalisa. Some people also read epics like the Ramayana and Mahabharata.

I had a super delicious dal ka halwa today. Sarla Aunty had called it dal ka seera. It is made from yellow dal and is just amazing.

13

VS Egg Hunt on Easter

The Kapoor house was so quiet, you could have heard a pin drop. Dadi was like a cat on a hot tin roof. Every time Dadu switched on the television, she started to fuss.

'You know that Nikhil gets distracted even by a bird outside the window, yet you are watching TV and that too a game as noisy as cricket,' she reprimanded her husband as though he were a three-year-old. 'Now Nikhil will keep popping out of the room on one pretext or another to see the score. By now he must have had five glasses of water. Either he is too thirsty, or he thinks I'm a fool.' She scowled at her grandson as he returned from the kitchen after quenching his thirst.

'Here,' she said, handing Nikhil two steel bottles. 'Now, until lunch is ready, I don't want to see you outside the room!' She wagged her finger in his face.

'Okay, Dadi, take it easy,' Nikhil said, making a face. 'By the time the exams are over, your blood pressure would have gone through the roof. I won't come out of the room until you call me.' He marched back to Natasha's room, his back rigid.

'I think I'll go to Sushil's house to watch the match,' Dadu said.

'That's a wonderful idea,' Dadi beamed. 'Why didn't I think of it before?'

'Because all the great ideas in this house come from me,' her husband said, grinning. 'In the meantime, you should do some deep-breathing exercises, or else, by the time the exams are over, you would have burst an artery.' Dadu closed the main door softly behind him.

A little later, the intercom rang. Lata picked up the receiver. 'Oh okay,' she said. 'I'll inform Madam.'

'Who was it?' Dadi whispered.

'Sarla Madam,' Lata said. 'She said that sir will have lunch with them.'

'Okay.' Dadi continued her crocheting.

Post lunch, Dadi went to her room to take a nap, leaving strict instructions with Lata to keep an eye on the twins as they studied together in Natasha's room.

'Dadi is more stressed about the exams then we are,' Nikhil joked.

'Yes, she scolded Lata for walking noisily and told her to walk barefoot,' Natasha added. 'I hope we do well in the exams, or Dadi will get more worked up.'

'You bet,' Nikhil said.

Shortly before 5 p.m., someone opened the main door softly. The twins heard hushed whispers. Nikhil looked wide-eyed at Natasha. 'I'm stopping myself from rushing out of this room only because of my concern for Dadi's health. I doubt Dadu can manage her elevated blood pressure.'

'Come out, kids,' Dadu called from the hall.

'Oh no!' Natasha exclaimed. 'All hell will break loose now.'

She darted out of the room, followed by her brother. Dadi emerged from her room, rubbing the sleep out of her eyes.

Dadu stood with Sushil Uncle in the living room. Sarla Aunty emerged from Lata's room.

'What is it? Why are you disturbing the children?' Dadi asked. 'Let them study.'

'Harmeet, you have said plenty of times that taking small breaks helps one's concentration and prevents boredom,' Dadu said cheerfully.

'Now what have you planned for us?' she raised her eyebrows.

'A treasure-hunt called VS Egg Hunt!' he grinned.

'VS?' Nikhil asked.

'Vinod–Sushil,' Sushil Uncle smiled. 'We have organized a small treasure hunt. We have hidden an Easter egg for each of you. We will give you the clues and all of you,' he pointed to the twins, Lata, his wife and Dadi, 'will have to go hunting.'

'The children have exams from tomorrow,' Dadi said. 'They are not going to waste time hunting for eggs.'

'Let them play, Harmeet,' Sarla Aunty said. 'It will be a welcome break for them.'

'Yes, dear,' Dadu coaxed his wife. 'It will just take half an hour.'

'Okay,' Dadi relented. 'But only for half an hour.'

'You have just twenty minutes to search for your clues. You should all look in your favourite places for your first clues,' Sushil Uncle instructed.

The five participants stared at each other in dismay. Which was their favourite place?

'Mine is easy,' Nikhil raced to his chair at the dining table. He looked beneath the chair. Tucked into a corner of the seat was a small piece of folded paper. He pulled it out and opened it. TELEVISION was written on it. He darted towards the TV in the living room. There was nothing there.

Natasha ran towards the fridge in the kitchen. Then she realized that the refrigerator was an object, not a place, and darted into the balcony, to the small swing sofa. She looked all around. Finally, she found her clue tucked into the yellow cushion. REFRIGERATOR was written on it. She confidently walked to the fridge and pulled it open.

In the shelf where the eggs were kept, she found her Easter egg.

There were three television sets in the house: the first in the living room, the second in the grandparents' room and the third in Lata's room. Nikhil sprinted into Lata's room and searched all around the TV. Behind the TV, in a small cardboard box, was his Easter egg.

Sarla Aunty walked into the puja room. As she lifted the folded mats, her piece of paper slipped out. LATA'S FAVOURITE PLACE was written on it. She smiled. This was easy. She ambled into the kitchen. On the counter was an overturned dish. She lifted it up and found a small cardboard box. Carrying her Easter egg, she strolled out of the kitchen.

Dadi and Lata were stuck, running helter-skelter searching for their favourite place or places in the house.

'Not fair,' Dadi said. 'Every nook and cranny of this house is my favourite place.'

'Same for me,' Lata grumbled.

'So you two are giving up, right?' Sushil Uncle asked.

'Sort of,' she replied.

'Either it's a yes or a no,' Dadu said.

'You still have four minutes left,' Sushil Uncle said, looking at his watch. 'If you two give up, then you have to share your Easter eggs with us. We could only get five.'

'We give up,' Dadi and Lata said, plonking themselves on the sofa where Nikhil, Natasha and Sarla Aunty were already halfway through their marzipan Easter eggs.

Dadi threw them a dirty look. 'Is no one here kind enough to at least offer me a bite?' she grumbled.

Dadu strolled out of the store room and Sushil Uncle out of the kitchen balcony. They each had a small, brown box in their hands.

'If you both had used your brains, you would have been the first to find the eggs,' Dadu said, breaking the yellow egg into two unequal pieces. Handing his wife the smaller part, he bit into the bigger piece.

Sushil Uncle made two equal halves. He offered Lata the first choice.

'Learn from your friend,' Dadi scowled at her husband.

Natasha's Journal

I don't know if the clues for the Easter egg hunt were easy, but I managed to find mine quickly and finished eating it fast too. Otherwise, I would have had to offer a bite to Dadi and Lata didi (I know I sound like Nikhil; I think his food-crazy behaviour is rubbing off on me!). Easter eggs are super yummy.

Easter, or Resurrection Sunday, is a Christian festival that celebrates the resurrection of Jesus Christ. According to the New Testament, it occurred on the third day of his burial after he was crucified. Easter is preceded by Lent, also called Great Lent, which is a period of fasting, penance and prayer that lasts for forty days. Dadu explained that many Christians refer to the week before Easter as the Holy Week. This Holy Week contains the days of the Easter Triduum, which is a period of three days. The Triduum includes Maundy Thursday, which commemorates the Maundy, or the washing of Jesus' feet, and the Last Supper; and Good Friday, which marks the crucifixion and death of Jesus. It also includes the Easter Vigil and the evening prayers on Easter Sunday. The Easter holiday does not fall on a fixed date in the Gregorian calendar.

During the Holy Week, Christians remember the final period in the life of Jesus, which started with his visit to Jerusalem and ended with his crucifixion.

My heart twisted with pain at the thought of what Jesus had undergone. When Dadu saw the sad expression on my face, he quickly changed the topic. He said Easter is also called Pascha.

Easter customs vary among Christians and could include early morning or sunrise services in church and wishing each other with the Paschal greeting, 'Christ is Risen!' Other customs include clipping the church, decorating Easter Eggs, egg hunting and Easter parade. Dadi said that an egg is the ancient symbol of new life and Easter eggs symbolize Jesus emerging from the tomb after his resurrection.

Dadu explained the meaning of clipping the church. He told us that this is an ancient custom that very few churches still follow. He said when the entire congregation of the church or the children hold hands and form an outward-facing circle around the church, it is called 'clipping the church'. And once this circle is completed, the crowd sings hymns and dances. I found this custom very sweet.

14

Dadu's Bihu Memories

'This is the second snake found in a Bengaluru apartment this month,' Dadu said while reading the newspaper in the morning.

'Don't even mention snakes,' Dadi shuddered. 'I get nightmares just thinking of them.'

'Do you remember the snake in our house, when we were posted in Assam?'

'How can I forget? It was Bihu, just like today,' Dadi said.

'Where was the snake?' Nikhil asked.

'The moment I opened my eyes, I saw a King Cobra sitting on our windowsill,' Dadu reminisced. 'Initially, I thought it was a dream. But then, a moment later, your grandmother woke up and saw it too.'

'What did you do, Dadu? Fight it?' Natasha asked.

Exchanging a look, their grandparents laughed.

'I'm sure he must have jumped out of bed and walked towards the snake! I can just see my brave, superman Dadu grabbing the snake by its neck and flinging it out of the window,' Nikhil grinned.

'Nothing so brave,' Dadu said apologetically. 'I screamed.'

'In fact, he screamed louder than me,' Dadi laughed. 'The army orderlies in the house thought we were being held hostage by terrorists. Sadly, they couldn't even barge into our room as our bedroom door was locked, and neither of us had the guts to get out of bed and open the door.'

'What did you do then?' Nikhil's eyes were wide with fear.

'You will laugh when we tell you what we did,' Dadu said.

'I rolled together your grandfather's socks and chucked the bundle at the snake,' Dadi said.

'Then the two of us ran to the bathroom and locked ourselves inside,' Dadu laughed, tears rolling down his cheeks.

'Before closing the bathroom door, I turned back to look at the snake,' Dadi said. 'The poor creature was swooning under the impact of your grandfather's socks, which I think he gives for a wash once a year on his birthday!'

'But my socks did come in handy to ward off the snake!' Dadu added, smiling.

'Luckily for us, our small bungalow had large, low windows – the old-fashioned kind,' Dadi explained, a faraway look in her eyes. 'We stood on the closed seat of the pot in the bathroom and climbed out of the window. Then we informed the orderlies who called a snake-catcher.'

'Then what happened?' Natasha asked.

'Your grandfather's socks had already weakened the snake! The snake-catcher entered the room through the bathroom window. He used the pillow cover on the bed to catch the snake. He later told us that he had expected the snake to put up a fight, but the snake was caught with minimum resistance,' she said.

'See, I told you my socks would one day turn out to be a strong weapon,' Dadu arched his eyebrows.

'You should have seen our neighbours' faces when they saw us crawling out of the bathroom window. They had all come to invite us for Bihu,' Dadi said.

'And what a Bihu it turned out to be!' Dadu said. 'We spent it in our neighbours' house, while the snake-catchers searched every nook and cranny of our house for the snake's family. Meanwhile, we gorged on pithas and larus.'

'Wait, I'll show you the photographs,' Dadi said. Removing a thick album from the last shelf of the cutlery cupboard in the living room, she flipped the pages until she arrived at the photo she was looking for.

Nikhil's Nook

Hi Friends,

I can't believe that my brave Dadu ran away instead of fighting the snake! But I think he did a sensible thing, because where snakes are concerned, bravery can be foolhardy. And although they had to be out of the house for a day, fortunately for them, they could spend it with people celebrating a festival – in this case, Bihu.

Bihu is one of Assam's major festivals. Like Baisakhi in Punjab and Vishu in Kerala, Bihu celebrates the crop cycle, particularly that of rice.

Turns out, Dadi was quite knowledgeable about this festival because of the day she spent with her neighbours a long time ago.

Bihu comprises three celebrations: Rongali Bihu, Kati Bihu and Bhogali Bihu, each of which is tied in with the crop cycle. Rongali Bihu is also called Bohag Bihu and Xaat Bihu. I find it difficult to pronounce Xaat. Rongali Bihu occurs in April and marks the beginning of the Assamese new year and the onset of spring.

Dadi told me that the most colourful of the three Bihu festivals is the Rongali Bihu or the spring festival, in which the celebrations continue for seven days, each of which is known by a different name: Chot Bihu, Goru Bihu, Manuh Bihu, Kutum Bihu, Senehi Bihu, Mela Bihu and Chera Bihu. Dadi rattled of the names like I would recite my Maths tables! At the time of Rongali Bihu, farmers have finished preparing the fields for the cultivation of paddy and everyone is in a celebratory mood.

Two Assamese traditional dishes are also prepared: pitha or rice cake, and larus made with rice and coconut. Both these dishes sound so tasty. Rongali Bihu is also a fertility festival: young women do the Bihu dance, which is called the Bihu Naas. Bihu folk songs or geet are also sung. There is music, dancing and feasting! There is also the tradition of hanging brass, copper or silver pots on poles in front of the house. Children wear flower garlands and go around the neighbourhood to wish everyone. This sounds like fun! No school, no restrictions!

Dadi also showed me the photograph of a unique musical instrument called pepa, which is made with the horn of a buffalo. The pepa is also played during Bihu.

Besides the fascinating pepa, there is also the xutuli. In the photo that Dadi showed me, it appeared like a rock with a small hole in the centre and two tiny holes on one side. The xutuli is played during Rongali Bihu. The crescent-shaped instrument is made from clay or the hollow part of the bamboo tree. Like Xaat Bihu, xutuli is another word I am not able to pronounce easily!

I'm hoping that Dadi makes pitha and larus for me.

15

The Twins'
Baisakhi Surprise

Dadi had made grand plans for a visit to Punjab once the twins' exams were over. She wanted the entire family to celebrate the Baisakhi festival with her brother. But Dadu's flu spoiled her plans. Halfway through the twins' exams, he caught the virus.

'Natasha, Nikhil, don't go into Dadu's room. The flu virus is contagious,' she warned the twins. She also forbade her husband from leaving his room. Throughout the duration of the exams, Dadu had been confined to his bedroom and even had his meals served to him there.

'I'll sleep in the hall,' Dadi told Lata, 'I don't want to carry the flu germs and transmit them to the three of you.'

Though Dadu and Lata tried to talk her into continuing with her trip, Dadi was determined to cancel the tickets, as she didn't want to leave her husband alone when he was sick.

'Madam, please take Nikhil and Natasha with you to Punjab. As soon as sir recovers, we will join you all there,' Lata tried to convince Dadi for the umpteenth time.

'No, Lata, it's okay,' Dadi said. 'I'll take the children to Punjab next year.'

'Go, Harmeet,' Dadu croaked. 'I'll manage, I'm not a kid.'

'Vinod, I won't be comfortable leaving you alone when you can barely talk,' Dadi said. She had already called the travel agent and cancelled the flight tickets. Though she was feeling sad, she put up a brave front.

The children's exams went off without a hitch, and Dadu recovered within a week. But sadly, the travel agent couldn't book fresh tickets for them as all the flights were full.

'I'm in no mood for any kind of Baisakhi celebrations tomorrow,' Dadi announced on the eve of the festival. Everyone stared at her in surprise. Taking care of her sick husband had taken a toll on Dadi, and she looked run down.

Early on Baisakhi day, Nikhil entered his sister's room, carrying the day's newspaper. 'Dadi is still sleeping in the hall,' he said. 'I think Dadu's cough disturbs her sleep at night.'

'Oh, I thought she must be awake,' Natasha said. 'I heard a sound in the kitchen.'

'That must be Lata didi, making tea and breakfast,' he replied. 'Hope she is making something interesting. I think it was the hunger pangs that woke me up so early.'

'Dadi was really looking forward to the trip. I wish we could do something to cheer her up,' Natasha said, staring absentmindedly at the paper her brother was flipping through. A small advertisement at the bottom caught her eye. 'Celebrity Chef Kunal Khanna's One Day Cooking Classes in Ivory Hotel. Entry Fee: Two thousand rupees per head. Lunch and high tea will be provided to all participants.' At the bottom was the contact number for registration.

'Are you reading what I'm reading?' Natasha said, her eyes bright with excitement.

'Yes,' Nikhil smiled. 'Cooking classes from Dadi's favourite chef. He is Sarla Aunty's favourite too.'

Picking up his phone from the bed, he dialled the number. 'Hello, I'm calling to ask about the cooking class registrations,' he said.

Natasha leaned close to her brother so she could hear what the voice on the other end was saying.

'Oh, oh,' he said. 'My grandmother won India's Innovative Chef Award. I want to surprise her.'

The lady said something. 'Oh, that will be cool,' Nikhil replied, a wide grin appearing on his face. 'Can you please reserve

two seats for my grandmother, Harmeet Kapoor, and her friend, Sarla Sadhwani?'

'What did the lady tell you?' Natasha asked after Nikhil had hung up.

'She said she will reserve two seats for me.'

'How do you know Sarla Aunty is free today?'

'She told me to bring Dadi over to her house, so that we all could play 'Snakes and Ladders' and 'Scrabble' together, as Sushil Uncle and Dadu will be gone the whole day for a snooker tournament.'

'That's cool,' Natasha said.

'I'll tell Sarla Aunty; you wake up Dadi,' he said and started walking towards the door.

'Nik, wait,' his sister said. 'It's our surprise, so we won't let them pay.' Running to her cupboard, she brought out her piggy bank. It was a digital piggy bank in the shape of a mosaic pig. After she clicked on the combination of numbers, the pig's bottom opened up. 'Thank God this is a new version. I hate to break my piggy bank every time I want to take out some money.'

'We can each pay half,' Nikhil said.

'Let's tell Dadi and Sarla Aunty, so that they both can get ready for the class,' Natasha said, looking at the paper. 'It starts at 11 a.m.'

Nikhil went to Sarla Aunty's flat to inform her, while Natasha walked into the hall to wake up her grandmother.

Dadi had just woken up and was sitting on the sofa-cum-bed with her head in her hands.

'Dadi, please get ready,' Natasha said. 'Nikhil and I have signed up Sarla Aunty and you for Celebrity Chef Kunal Khanna's One Day Cooking Classes in Ivory Hotel.'

'What?' Dadi sat up straight.

Natasha showed her the advertisement. 'But, Dadi,' she said, 'Nikhil and I are going to pay for the cooking course for you and Sarla Aunty.'

'No, no, neither I nor Sarla would like the idea of the two of you paying for this course,' Dadi said. She looked up at the clock. It was 7:45 a.m.

'Sorry, Dadi, you either accept our condition or be happy seeing Kunal Khanna on TV,' Natasha said firmly.

'We will discuss all that later,' Dadi ran into her bedroom. 'Tell Lata to keep my tea ready. And have you informed Sarla?'

'Nikhil has gone to inform Aunty,' Natasha said.

At 10 a.m., the twins got into the car with the two excited ladies. Muniraju stared open-mouthed at the two women, as they got into the back seat with Natasha. Nikhil sat in the passenger seat beside the driver.

'Going for a wedding?' he asked, turning the key in the ignition.

Dadi and Sarla Aunty were dressed in their best clothes and carried matching clutch purses. They had both applied make-up and styled their hair.

'Everything Kunal Khanna does comes on television,' Dadi explained. 'So one should be ready to be on camera.'

'Yes,' Sarla Aunty nodded in agreement. 'Better prepared than caught unawares. Harmeet, I told Nikhil that I won't let him pay for the course,' Sarla Aunty said. Opening her clutch, she pulled out her compact to refresh her lipstick for the fourth time.

'Dadi, Sarla Aunty, we are doing this for ourselves,' Nikhil turned around in his seat. 'I'm sure you will make all of Chef Kunal Khanna's dishes for us. So, in short, we are doing this for our stomachs!'

Neither Dadi nor Sarla Aunty had a reply to this sound logic.

Natasha's Journal

I felt bad for Dadi as our trip to Punjab had not worked out. Nikhil and I decided to cheer her up because we didn't want her to spend Baisakhi moping at home. I think it was pure luck that I saw Celebrity Chef Kunal Khanna's advertisement in the newspaper. The registration for the cooking course could have been a problem, but Nikhil managed to reserve two seats for Dadi and Sarla Aunty (who we both love as much as Dadi) by mentioning that Dadi was the winner of the Innovative Chef Award. This was our Baisakhi treat for them.

Baisakhi is the harvest festival of Punjab as well as the new year. Baisakhi is also called Vaisakhi or Vasakhi. It is celebrated on the first day of the Vaisakh month of the Sikh calendar. This day corresponds with either April 13 or 14 in the Gregorian calendar.

Farmers celebrate Baisakhi by thanking god for the abundant harvest and praying for a good crop in the coming year. Dadu told me about a few traditions associated with Baisakhi. One of them was the Aawat Pauni, in which people gather in big groups to harvest the wheat to the beat of drums. He told me that the Baisakhi festival is important for Sikhs as it was on Baisakhi day in 1699 that the Tenth Guru of the Sikhs, Guru Gobind Singh, established the Panth Khalsa or the Order of the Pure Ones. Sikhs who accept the five Ks in their lives do so on Baisakhi day. The five Ks symbolize one's commitment to the Panth and to the Sikh way of life. They are Kesh (uncut hair), Kangha (wooden comb), Kara (an iron bracelet), Kachera (cotton undergarment) and Kirpan (a small dagger).

Bhangra, one of the most popular folk dances of Punjab, is a vibrant and vigorous traditional harvest dance that captures the celebratory spirit of Baisakhi.

Baisakhi fairs are held in many places, and people eat the delicious sarson ka saag (which I can assure you is the yummiest green vegetable you can ever eat) along with makki ki roti. There is also my all-time favourite – chole-bhature. (I had three small bhaturas last week, and as usual, Nikhil beat me by having four.)

I'm sure Nikhil is hoping that Dadi and Sarla Aunty will cook more yummy food after attending Chef Kunal Khanna's cookery course. My brother can never take his mind off food.

16

Potluck on Poila Baishak

The registration process for the Cooking Classes was relatively easy. After the twins paid the entry fee, Dadi and Sarla Aunty received their entry cards. A few cameramen thronged the entrance of the room where the cooking classes were being conducted.

Sarla Aunty and Dadi stood stiffly when the cameramen asked them to pose.

'Relax,' Nikhil said. 'You two aren't being punished.'

'Be good children, don't trouble your teacher,' Natasha said and winked.

Holding hands, the two ladies entered the room.

'They were so nervous,' Nikhil laughed as they exited the hotel.

Muniraju brought the car to the entrance. 'Where to now?' he asked.

'To Arbaaz's house,' Nikhil said. 'We will spend some time with them and return home for lunch.'

Arbaaz and Amina Aziz were Nikhil and Natasha's

classmates and fraternal twins, just like them!

'Okay. Two festivals today: Baisakhi and Poila Baishak, which is the Bengali New Year. That's why such little traffic today,' Muniraju said as he put the car in second gear. 'I like driving on the roads when there is less traffic.'

As he turned into the lane that led to their house, they saw Amina and Arbaaz walking up the road.

'Your friends are coming to meet you,' Muniraju said, bringing the car to a halt.

'Hey, we were coming to see you,' Amina said as the twins got out of the car. Both Amina and her brother were fair-skinned with long eyelashes and thick black hair. The only difference was the shape of their faces and the length of their hair. Amina had an oval face and her long hair was tied in a ponytail, while Arbaaz had a round face and short hair with a neat side parting.

'What a coincidence!' Nikhil smiled. 'We were coming to see you.'

'Let's go for ice-cream,' Arbaaz said.

The four friends started walking down the road to the ice-cream parlour two lanes away.

'Hey, that looks like Sharbani Ma'am,' Natasha said, pointing to a woman emerging from an auto. Their teacher was wearing a traditional white sari with a red border, and her long hair was in a bun encircled by a string of white flowers.

Sharbani Basu was their Maths teacher. She was the youngest teacher in school and one of the nicest. She never scolded or punished any of her students.

As she removed her bags from the auto, the four friends ran towards her.

'Sharbani Ma'am,' Natasha said, rushing forward to help her.

'What a pleasant surprise!' their teacher smiled. 'What are the four of you doing here?'

'We live in this lane,' Amina said.

'You look very pretty,' Natasha said.

'Shubho Nabo Barsho,' Arbaaz wished their teacher.

'Shubho Nabo Barsho to you all,' Sharbani Ma'am smiled.

Natasha and Amina exchanged a look when they saw Nikhil and Arbaaz blush.

'What are you doing here, Ma'am?' Natasha asked.

'I've rented an apartment in this building,' their teacher replied.

'We will help you carry your stuff.' Natasha picked up two cloth bags, one containing vegetables, the other a few steel plates and spoons.

Carrying one large bag herself, Sharbani Ma'am led them into the foyer of the building. Then she turned right, as her apartment was on the ground floor.

'Be careful; don't step on my alpana,' she said, as they approached her flat.

They all looked at her with puzzled expressions on their faces.

'Rangolis are called alpanas in Bengali,' she explained, pointing to the elaborate pattern she had drawn outside her flat.

'It's beautiful,' Amina said.

'How long did it take you to make this?' Natasha asked.

'Nearly two hours,' their teacher replied.

'Are you spending your new year alone?' Amina asked.

'I had planned to go to Kolkata to spend Poila Baishak with my parents, but sadly, I didn't get permission. Principal Ma'am wanted me to finish correcting the exam papers.' Their teacher made a sad face. 'Since I'm new to Bengaluru, I don't know anyone here.'

'Ma'am, can we spend Poila Baishak with you?' Natasha asked. 'I'll get lunch from my house, and we will all eat with you. My Dadi says no one should spend their festival alone. It's not right that you are spending your new year all by yourself.'

'I can't let you do that,' their teacher said.

'No, Ma'am,' Amina said. 'Please let us spend the new year with you. I'll get some food from my house too.'

'Okay,' Sharbani Ma'am agreed. 'I'll arrange for ice creams and sweets,' she said.

They all met half an hour later. Natasha and Nikhil had bought sarson ka saag and makki ki roti as well as chole-bhature. Amina and Arbaaz came with vegetable biryani and cutlets. And Sharbani Ma'am opened two boxes of rasgullas and mishti doi. She had also ordered chocolate ice cream.

While Amina and Natasha helped their teacher lay out the food, Arbaaz and Nikhil arranged the plates and cutlery.

'This is the best potluck I've ever had,' Sharbani Ma'am said.

Nikhil's Nook

Hi Friends,

Sharbani Ma'am is our Maths teacher, and she is the sweetest teacher I've ever had. It was a pleasant surprise to see her in our area. I can't believe that she will be living nearby. I'm glad she agreed when we insisted that we spend the afternoon with her. It was the yummiest potluck I've ever had. And I feel she enjoyed our company as much as we enjoyed hers.

Sharbani Ma'am told us that Poila Baishak or Pohela Boishakh is the Bengali New Year. It is the first day of the Bengali Calendar and falls around mid-April. Sharbani Ma'am said that the Bengali New Year begins at the crack of dawn. She told us that, as a child, she would accompany her grandfather for the early morning processions or Prabhat Pheries. The day is celebrated with processions and fairs. Traditionally, businesses and traders start this day with a new ledger or account book. Flowers, garlands and mango leaves are used to decorate shops, business establishments and markets. It is also believed to be a favourable day to start new ventures.

Ma'am gave us an interesting detail about her life – her parents got married on Poila Baishak twenty-eight years ago. The entire month is considered auspicious for marriages.

One of the popular traditions associated with the day is the making of elaborate rangolis—or alpanas as Sharbani Ma'am called them—in front of the house.

She also explained that she was dressed in traditional Bengali attire, which consisted of a white sari with a red border accompanied by flowers in the hair. Men wore dhoti-kurta on this day. According to Sharbani Ma'am, in villages, it is a tradition to perform and watch classical plays called jatras on Poila Baishak.

She also told us that the new year feast must have fish and mutton, along with mishti doi.

I have become a big fan of mishti doi. It was love at first taste when I had my first spoonful!

I forgot to ask Arbaaz how he knew that on Poila Baishak Bengalis greet each other with 'Shubho Nabo Barsho', which means Happy New Year.

17

Lata's Vishukkani

The twins had returned home from the delicious potluck they had shared with Sharbani Ma'am and their friends, Amina and Arbaaz. There was no news of Dadi or Dadu.

Lata was fluttering around the house like an excited bee, darting from one room to another, gathering an assortment of objects and carrying them to her room.

'What's up, Lata didi?' Nikhil asked. 'Why are you carrying so many things to your room? Do you need my help?'

'No, dear,' Lata said. 'Give me five minutes.'

She joined them in the living room a little later. 'How was your lunch potluck?'

'Super,' the twins replied.

'But why are you shifting half the house into your room?' Nikhil asked again.

'Not shifting, arranging my Vishukkani,' she said.

'What is that?' Natasha frowned.

'I'll show you,' Lata led them into her room.

In one corner of the room, on a small wooden platform, stood an idol of Lord Krishna that Lata had brought in from the puja room. Beside it was a small idol of Lord Ganesha. A brand new white bedsheet was spread on the ground, on which Lata had placed several banana leaves. On one leaf was fruit – a bunch of bananas, grapes, an apple, a mango, a papaya and a coconut broken into two halves; on the second leaf was an assortment of vegetables – drumsticks, a small jackfruit, carrots, pumpkin, ladyfingers and beans. On the third leaf were new notes of different denominations, each held in place by a newly minted coin. A silver coin with Lakshmi engraved on it was placed on top.

'I'll light the agarbattis and the lamp tomorrow,' Lata said, pointing to the agarbatti holder next to the idol of Krishna. A copy of the Ramayana lay on another leaf. It was like the one Sarla Aunty had gifted the twins. On the same leaf was a new diary. Two new spatulas—one steel and the other wooden—were kept on top of the diary.

'An uruli is the most important item of the Kani,' Lata said, pointing to the last leaf on which was kept a circular brass dish filled with uncooked rice.

She balanced a yellow cucumber on the bed of rice and put a metallic mirror inside it so that they could see their reflection in it. Then she placed the uruli in front of Krishna's idol and decorated it with a garland of yellow flowers. 'It is believed that Konna flowers bloom during Vishu,' she said, holding a yellow flower in her hand.

Straightening a few items, she said, 'The diary is my recipe book. As a child, I would keep my textbook and pen. Now, I keep my recipe book and spatulas.'

'So much stuff,' Natasha said. She looked wide-eyed at the banana leaves.

'This is my Vishukkani,' Lata explained. 'In Malayalam the word 'Kani' means 'that which is seen first.' So Vishukkani means 'that which is seen first on Vishu day.' Our Kani consists of items or objects we want to see on Vishu morning. This tradition arises from the belief that good things seen on New Year's Day become a lucky charm, bringing good fortune for the whole year. Vishu is not just our new year, it also signifies the start of our harvest season.'

'Amazing!' Nikhil said.

'I like to see these items first thing on Vishu morning,' Lata smiled. 'It brings me good luck for the entire year.'

'I want to do the same tomorrow,' Natasha said.

'Me too,' Nikhil said.

'Okay,' Lata agreed. 'I'll wake you up and close your eyes and bring you to the Kani, so that this is the first thing you both see in the morning.'

'Lata didi, can I add something to your Kani?' Natasha asked.

'Sure.'

Natasha ran to her room and returned carrying two photographs, one of her parents and the other a group picture of Dadu, Dadi, Sushil Uncle, Sarla Aunty, Lata, Nikhil and herself. She placed the photos on top of Lata's recipe book.

The next day, Lata woke up bright and early. After she had looked at her Kani, she went to Natasha's room and, holding her hand over Natasha's eyes, led her into the room to see the Kani.

'First, look at the idol of Krishna; then see your reflection in the mirror,' Lata said.

Leaving Natasha in her room, she led Nikhil inside,

keeping her hand over his eyes. She repeated the same instructions for Nikhil.

Later, after getting dressed, the twins joined Lata as she lit the brass lamps and the agarbattis. Lata gifted Natasha a yellow kurti and Nikhil a blue kurta.

Dadi had bought a purple silk sari for Lata, which she made the twins present to her.

Natasha's Journal

I love this tradition of Vishukanni. Though I didn't assemble one, I kept a few things precious to me in Lata didi's Kani. Nikhil added more things than I did. After dinner, I saw him putting his iPad, laptop and a ladle on two banana leaves.

Lata didi gave me lots of information related to Vishu. Vishu is the New Year for the people of Kerala and is celebrated in the month of Medam, which falls around mid-April in the Gregorian calendar. I started writing in my journal while she was talking about Vishukanni, which she said is an arrangement of objects or things that people want to see on waking up on Vishu day. One must keep one's eyes closed till one reaches the Kani. This tradition comes from the belief that the auspicious objects one sees on Vishu morning will continue throughout the year. Lata didi explained this in a very beautiful way. She said that as a child, she was asked to look at the idol of Lord Krishna and then see her own reflection in the Valkannadi (a mirror made of metal). This was to remind people that god (or divinity) exists within us and that we must show love and respect to others as everyone has the divine within them. She further explained that looking into a mirror is also symbolic of trying to look within and clear our negative thoughts. I like the thought behind this tradition.

According to Lata didi, one of the interesting beliefs associated with Vishu is that it was only after Ravana's death that the Sun began to rise from the east again. So, this festival signifies the return of the Sun to its usual direction.

Lata didi said that Vishu is also the festival of light and fireworks. Among other traditions was the buying and wearing of new clothes, which she referred to as Puthukodi, and the giving of money or Vishukkaineetam by the elders of the family to the youngsters, in the form of newly minted coins. Lata didi gave Nikhil and me a five-hundred-rupee note and a one-rupee coin.

And then there is the special feast or Sadya, which consists of equal proportions of salty, sour, bitter and sweet food.

18

Akshaya Tritiya
with a Twist

'Oh no,' Dadi groaned as she looked at the newspaper Dadu was reading at the dining table. They had just finished their breakfast of puri, aloo ki sabzi and boondi raita. 'Thanks to the stress of Nikhil and Natasha's exams and supervising their studies, I completely forgot to make my usual sherbet for Akshaya Tritiya. And I have to chair the meeting of the committee members of the building in the absence of the committee President, Mr Rao, who is in Mumbai.'

'Don't worry, dear,' Dadu said. 'You can skip this year.'

'No, no,' Dadi said. 'I doubt I'll have the time today.' Then turning to Lata, she said, 'You will have to undertake this task.'

'No!' Lata trembled, as though Dadi had asked her to jump into a lion's cage. 'I've never been able to master these tricky sherbets. My sugar syrup is either too thin or too thick. After it crystallized last year, I don't have the guts to make it again. Please forgive me, Madam.' She ran out of the room before Dadi could stop her.

'Why do you want to make the sherbet, Dadi?' Natasha asked.

'When we were in Indore as newly-weds, a Sindhi neighbour would make sherbet on Akshaya Tritiya and distribute it to the building staff and to the children of the nearby slums. I would help her as she had arthritis and couldn't make the sherbet alone. Ever since then, I've been following this tradition. For the last thirty years, I have been distributing sherbet to the building staff and the children from the nearby slums on this day. I don't want to break the ritual this year.' Dadi's face fell.

'Can I suggest something, Dadi?' Nikhil said. 'Instead of sherbet, why don't we buy small packs of juice and distribute them to the building staff and the children from the slums?'

'What a wonderful idea,' Dadi smiled. 'This way, I'll still be following my tradition and the staff and children will get their treat. Why didn't I think of that?' She smacked her head with her hand. 'Come here,' she said to Nikhil.

Nikhil walked towards his grandmother.

'Thank you,' she said and kissed his cheek.

'This way, Dadi, you will also be helping Satheji move into a bigger shop,' he said. 'Remember you blessed him on his inauguration that he would soon have a much bigger shop. You constantly complain that people are either buying stuff in supermarkets or online, and this is affecting the small shop owners who are barely surviving, so by buying from them you will be helping them.'

Dadi nodded. 'Wait, let me give you some money.' She went into her room, emerging a few seconds later with two five-hundred-rupee notes. 'Buy fifty fruit juices and fifty pieces of Mysore pak,' she said. 'I've made a list of all the building staff, and asked the driver to call the children from the slums. Lata will take you around later, and both you and Natasha can distribute it together,' she said.

Lata accompanied the twins to Satheji's shop down the road. Satheji was delighted to see them.

'Welcome, welcome,' he said.

He looked pleased when they picked up fifty small packs of fruit juice and fifty pieces of Mysore pak. He gave them a five per cent discount and chatted with them while he packed the juices and sweets in cloth bags.

'It's hot. Here, drink this.' He handed them three apple juices.

'Let us pay you for these,' Lata said, opening her wallet.

'No, no,' he shook his hands. 'These are for you three from my side.'

'Thank you,' the twins said together.

Loaded with their goods, they walked back home.

'Sweet of him to give us free juice,' Natasha said.

'Yeah,' Nikhil nodded, sipping his juice.

'Where will you find the slum dwellers' children?' Natasha asked the housekeeper.

'Madam and Sarla Madam usually feed the children lunch on certain festivals. Muniraju will convey the message to one of the elders in the slum, and that person will bring all the children to our building,' Lata said. 'Sarla Madam is very active in social causes; she is also very helpful. Only her singing voice can scare ghosts.' Lata grinned.

'You heard us,' Nikhil said.

'I was dusting outside the room when you two were talking,' she explained.

'Dadi is right, even walls have ears.' Nikhil made a face.

They all laughed. Sarla Aunty was standing in the balcony of her flat, talking on her mobile phone. She waved to them. They all waved back.

'Nikhil, I've made some kaju katli for you,' Sarla Aunty said. 'Pick it up when you are free.'

As they entered their building compound, they saw that Muniraju had assembled a motley group of people: both the slum dwellers and the building staff.

Natasha distributed the Mysore pak, while Nikhil gave out the juice.

Nikhil's Nook

Hi Friends,

First, let me tell you that Dadi loved my idea of distributing juice, instead of sherbet, to the children from the nearby slum on Akshaya Tritiya.

Akshaya Tritiya, also known as Akti or Akha Teej, is an annual spring festival, which falls in April or May in the Gregorian calendar.

Lata didi explained that in Sanskrit, the word 'Akshaya' means 'eternal or never-diminishing' and links up with the wish for unending prosperity, hope, success and happiness. Tritya means 'third' and is named after the 'third lunar day' of the month of Vaisakha in the Hindu calendar. It is believed that Parsuram, the sixth incarnation of Vishnu was born on Akshaya Tritiya.

Hindus and Jains consider Akshaya Tritiya as an auspicious day to perform marriage ceremonies, or to invest in gold, diamonds or property. In fact, the day is considered so auspicious that you don't need a mahurat or an auspicious time to start a new venture or for any special ceremony. People also carry out charitable activities as it is supposed to bring prosperity and good luck to the family. It is also a day for remembering the people who have passed away in the family. According to legend, Veda Vyasa began to recite the Mahabharata to Ganesha on this day.

Natasha and I researched the connection of sherbet and juice to Akshaya Tritiya. Followers of Jainism also consider Akshaya Tritiya as an auspicious day. It is associated with Lord Adinatha, also known as Rishabhadeva, the first of the twenty-four Tirthankaras. Many Jains keep a Varshi-tap or fast on alternate days for an entire year. They finish their year-long tapasya by drinking sugarcane juice. Hence the connection between the festival and juice or sherbet. People prepare traditional Indian sweets like halwa, kheer, barfi and offer these to Lord Vishnu.

Throughout the day Dadi had been grumbling that the essence of festivals was getting lost. She felt that festivals are about making sure everyone celebrated equally, but with the current marketing trends that tended to glamourize festivals, it was now also about accumulating material possessions and buying gold and diamonds specially on festivals like Akshaya Tritiya.

The children from the slum and the building staff were delighted with their Akshaya Tritiya treat. I really appreciate Dadi's gesture of making the less fortunate a part of her celebrations.

And I hope you all are enjoying the change in my writing style. (I hope I'm not sounding like my sister Natasha, though I have a feeling that she is copying my writing style as she can read my blog while I can't read her journal.)

And Sarla Aunty's kaju katli was out of this world. She also sent me some aate ke laddoo. She later told me that the trick is to roast the wheat flour in such a way that the laddoo doesn't stick to the palate when people eat it. These laddoos were light, tasty and healthy.

19

Passing on the Goodness on Buddha Purnima

As planned, Reema and Raunak Rao met the twins in the building compound. When the twins had first seen Reema, they were enchanted by her elfin face and her hair that was cut in an inverted bob. Reena was always dressed in printed bermudas and dark coloured t-shirts and constantly chewed gum. Compared to his thirteen-year-old sister, Raunak, older by sixteen months, was soft-spoken, with hair that was neatly parted at the side. Like Natasha and Nikhil, the Rao siblings also stayed with their grandparents as their parents were working overseas in Singapore.

The four had been playing badminton for half an hour when Nikhil saw the new boy. Thin and short, with hair cropped close to his scalp, the boy seemed around eleven to twelve years old and was standing in the corner watching them play. He had a wide-eyed look on his face, as he stared at the children playing in the compound.

'Must be from the family that has just moved into flat 1C,' Nikhil said to Natasha.

'Ya, Sarla Aunty said they seem to be a very quiet family; not a sound is to be heard from their flat,' Natasha replied.

'Where are they from?' he asked.

'I don't remember whether she said Sikkim or Arunachal Pradesh.' Natasha looked at the boy as he lowered his head shyly and quickly moved towards the group of children playing cricket.

'We don't need an extra player,' Ravi said loudly, waving his bat almost threateningly at the boy. He was tall and well built, with curly hair and a permanent scowl on his face.

The boy returned to his place with a crestfallen look on his face.

Nikhil headed towards him. The boy stared at him fearfully.

'Hi, I'm Nikhil,' he introduced himself. 'What's your name?'

'Pema Pongen,' he replied softly, as though speaking to himself.

'Want to take my place?' Nikhil offered, holding out his badminton racket. 'I'm tired, I could do with some water and rest.'

Pema eagerly accepted the racket and joined Natasha. The game turned furious as Raunak engaged Pema in a volley, which the new boy won.

'Hey, you are good!' Raunak shook his hand. 'Where did you learn to play?'

'In school, from our P.T. teacher,' Pema replied.

Nikhil introduced Pema Pongen to everyone.

'Where are you from?' Natasha asked.

'Sikkim,' Pema said. 'I'm a Buddhist.'

'Wow, I've never met a Buddhist before,' Reema said. 'I read in the newspaper that today is Buddha Purnima,' she said. 'Happy Buddha Purnima, Pema,' she wished him.

'Happy Buddha Purnima,' the others too wished him.

'Thank you,' he said shyly.

'How do you celebrate your festival?' Natasha asked.

Ever since she had started her journal, her curiosity had increased. She wanted to learn about the various customs and rituals associated with each festival.

'Since we have moved here recently, we don't know if there is a Buddhist temple in the city. So we placed our statue of Buddha in a basin filled with water and decorated it with flowers. My mother says that this symbolizes a new beginning.'

'That's so sweet,' Natasha smiled.

After playing for an hour, they ended the game as it had become

dark. No one wanted to return home yet, so they decided to sit and chat in the building lobby.

'Wait, I'll show you my album,' Pema said. He ran upstairs to his flat and returned a few minutes later with a fat album.

'This is a photo of the Tawang Monastery in Arunachal Pradesh. It's the largest monastery in India and the second largest in the world,' he said proudly. 'I've visited it many times when I was small.'

'It looks beautiful,' Reema sighed. 'I would love to visit it.'

'Me too,' Natasha nodded.

'Sikkim is so beautiful,' Raunak said, as they flipped through the album.

'Do you have any siblings?' Natasha asked.

'I'm an only child,' he replied softly.

'Now you have four new friends,' Nikhil smiled.

Pema nodded shyly.

A little later, they all broke up as dinner time was approaching.

'We met the new boy – Pema Pongen,' Natasha said at the dining table.

'I saw from the balcony,' Dadi said. 'Nikhil, it was sweet of you to invite him to play with you all.'

'When I saw that wherever Pema was going, he was being snubbed by the building children, I felt bad for him. Then I remembered how Arbaaz had saved me from being bullied in school and I decided to talk to Pema so that he didn't feel like an outsider,' Nikhil said.

'After we asked him to join us, everyone wanted to play with Pema,' Natasha laughed. 'He is quiet and shy too.'

'You did a good thing, Nikhil,' their grandmother said and smiled. 'I'm proud of you. One must always be gracious and kind, no matter what the circumstances. I'm planning to take some sweets and ask Sarla to accompany me to welcome the Pongens to our society.'

Natasha's Journal

I was disappointed seeing our building children's behaviour towards Pema. It was mean of them to snub Pema when he wanted to join their games. At that moment, I remembered our first day in Goodwin Convent school and the way Nikhil and I felt awkward because no one wanted to befriend us. If Arbaaz hadn't come and sat with Nikhil and Amina hadn't constantly borrowed my stuff, I doubt that the rest of the class would have warmed up to us or that we would have adjusted so fast or so well.

I'm glad Nikhil took the first step to making Pema comfortable. And it was Pema's festival too. I've never met a Buddhist. All I knew about Buddhists was that they worshipped Buddha.

Buddha Purnima is also called Vesak or Buddha Jayanti. It is a Buddhist festival celebrated on the full moon day of the Hindu month of Vaisakha, which is April or May in the Gregorian calendar. It is believed that Lord Buddha was born on a full moon day in the month of Vaisakha and that Buddha achieved both enlightenment and nirvana, which means salvation, on this day.

After dinner, Dadi told us about Gautama Buddha. He was born as Siddhartha Gautama in Lumbini in Nepal. His father Suddhodhana Tharu was the king of Kapilvastu and his mother was Maya Devi. Siddhartha lived a sheltered life in the palace, far away from the hardships and miseries of the world. He therefore had no idea about sickness, disease, old age or death. When Siddhartha was sixteen years old, his father got him married to Yashodhara. Siddhartha and Yashodhara had a son called Rahul. One day, while Siddhartha was travelling through his kingdom on a chariot, he saw an old man, a man with a disease and a dead body. Seeing these images of worldly suffering, Siddhartha began to wonder about the nature of the world—about misery, suffering and old age—and decided to leave his life of comfort in the palace and pursue the path of knowledge instead. It is believed that after years of meditation, he attained Enlightenment and became Buddha or the 'Awakened One'. Buddha attained enlightenment under a fig or Bodhi tree. During his meditation, Buddha found answers to the Four Noble Truths – that all life is suffering, that suffering is caused by meaningless desires, that these desires can be destroyed, that the means to achieve this desire-free state devoid of suffering is to follow the eightfold path. The principles of this path are right understanding, right thought, right speech, right conduct, right means of making a living, right mental attitude, right mindfulness and right concentration. Buddhism is founded on Buddha's teachings.

Dadi explained to me the concept of the Dharma wheel or Dharmachakra, a wooden wheel with eight spokes that represents Buddha's teachings on the path to enlightenment. The eight spokes stand for the eightfold path of Buddhism. On Buddha Purnima, people visit Buddhist temples, listen to sermons, recite Buddhists scriptures and meditate. People also offer fruits and flowers to statues of Lord Buddha. Some temples follow the ritual that Pema had told us about, that of placing a small statue of the infant Buddha in a basin of water and decorating it with flowers. Visitors then pour water over this statue to symbolize a new beginning.

Pema told us that some people participate in charitable activities and some free captive animals as a symbol of compassion for all living creatures.

I would love to set a caged animal or bird free!

20

Eid Mubarak, Amina and Arbaaz

Ever since the Aziz twins, Amina and Arbaaz, had invited Nikhil and Natasha for Eid lunch, Nikhil couldn't stop thinking about all the food he would eat there – specially the biryani and seviyan.

The four had several common interests and had bonded over the last couple of months, more so because they were two sets of twins! While Nikhil and Arbaaz shared a common interest in food and computers, Natasha and Amina bonded over books. Arbaaz and Amina had helped the twins get a grip on the syllabus as well, especially because they had joined the school mid-term. This was the second time Arbaaz and Amina had kept a Roza or fast during the holy month of Ramadan, also called Ramzan.

'I still remember the day the four of us first became friends at school,' Nikhil said as they sat together in Natasha's room. 'Do you remember we were sitting under the Guava tree in a large group? The moment we opened our lunch boxes, I saw Arbaaz eyeing my chole-bhature. When I turned to him, he pretended he was looking at the tree. I offered to share my lunch with him. He immediately handed me his chapati and chicken and grabbed my lunch box,' Nikhil laughed.

'That sealed our friendship with them,' Natasha smiled. 'I think Amina has eaten from my tiffin box more than I have eaten from it!'

'Yes!' Nikhil grinned. 'Our puri-sabzi, aloo paratha and pav-bhaji are their favourites.'

'Don't forget the gulab jamuns,' Natasha said and laughed. 'In fact, if you and Amina ever have a gulab-jamun eating competition, she might even beat you!'

'That reminds me, Lata didi has made gulab jamuns for us to take to their house for Eid lunch today,' he said.

'Cool,' Natasha said.

'I'll always be grateful to Arbaaz for saving me from the bullies,' Nikhil said. 'I still shudder at the memory of the time they had cornered me in the restroom. Fortunately for me, Arbaaz entered the room just then and told them not to trouble me,' Nikhil said.

'He is a great guy,' Natasha smiled. 'Always ready to help people.' Looking at her watch, she said, 'I think we need to start getting dressed; it's nearly 12 p.m. Amina said to come early.'

'You are right,' Nikhil said. 'It will take me time to wear the churidar, since this will be my first time in one,' he looked worried. 'Will I be able to eat with the tight waistband of the churidar around my waist?' he frowned.

'Don't worry, it's easy to wear and comfortable too,' Natasha said. 'It's just like jeggings, with two hooks at the bottom.'

Nikhil left to get dressed, closing the door softly behind him.

Fifteen minutes later, Natasha stood before the mirror, staring at her reflection. She had worn a pink silk salwar-kurta with a pale-pink dupatta draped around her neck.

After a brief knock on her door, Nikhil entered the room. He was wearing a pale-yellow kurta over a cream-coloured silk churidar.

He couldn't stop staring at his reflection. 'This colour is super. Sarla Aunty has amazing taste,' he said.

'Yes, I love this shade,' Natasha said. 'She always gives us great gifts.'

'Let's click a picture to send Mom and Dad,' she said.

'Great idea.'

Sarla Aunty entered the room carrying something in her hand. 'I forgot to give you this,' she said. She then removed a bindi from the packet and stuck it in the centre of Natasha's forehead. 'Now your dress is complete,' she said. 'You look like a doll!'

'What about me?' Nikhil asked.

'My prince!' She put her arms around the children.

'Aunty, can you click a picture, we want to send it to Mom and Dad,' Natasha said.

Sarla Aunty clicked half a dozen pictures on Natasha's phone and handed it back to her.

'Now one with you,' Nikhil said with a smile.

Natasha took a selfie and immediately sent the photographs to her parents.

Dadi entered the room and, seeing the twins dressed in traditional attire, nodded in approval. She handed them two gift-wrapped boxes for the Aziz twins. Nikhil carried the two boxes in his hand, while Natasha held the steel container with the gulab jamuns. The Kapoor twins set out for their friends' house in the next lane.

It was a pleasant day – a cool breeze moved around lazily. Within a few minutes, they reached the Aziz bungalow. The door was open. Several guests were entering the house.

The moment Arbaaz and Amina saw the twins, they ran towards them. Amina was in a blue and

gold sharara, while Arbaaz wore a brocade sherwani and cream churidar.

'Eid Mubarak,' the Kapoor twins wished.

'Shukriya.' Their friends hugged them.

'For you,' they said, handing over the gifts to their friends.

'Thank you,' the Aziz siblings replied, graciously accepting the presents and keeping them aside on a table nearby.

'Come meet Ami and Abu.' Their friends dragged them into the living room, where their parents were greeting relatives.

'Eid Mubarak, Aunty, Uncle,' Natasha and Nikhil wished them together.

'Thank you,' the senior Azizs said warmly. Mr Aziz was tall and slim, with translucent skin like his children, and hair that was slightly longer than Arbaaz's and curled at the edges. His beige pathani suit had a light sprinkling of silk embroidery on the sleeves.

'I'm happy you could join us for lunch,' Mrs Aziz said with a smile, revealing two dimples on her oval face. She looked beautiful in a red-and-gold salwar-kurta, her long hair tied in a loose plait and her brown eyes large and shiny.

The Kapoor twins were led into the dining room by their friends. This was the moment Nikhil had been waiting for so eagerly! The table was loaded with large dishes of chicken biryani, mutton kebabs, chicken tikkas, egg cutlets, raita and seviyan.

Needless to say, Nikhil had second helpings of everything.

After the lunch was over, they chatted with their friends' cousins. The Azizs lived in a joint family.

'Abu is calling you both,' Amina said a little later.

The Kapoor twins weaved through the crowd in the living room.

Mr Aziz held two gold-coloured envelopes in his hand. 'Eidi for you both,' he smiled at them.

'No, no ...' But before Nikhil could complete his sentence, Mr Aziz interrupted. 'You are just like Arbaaz and Amina for us. If you say no, I'll feel hurt.'

Exchanging a look, the Kapoor twins accepted the golden envelopes.

'Thank you, uncle,' they said.

Nikhil's Nook

Hi Friends,

I enjoyed my Eid lunch with Amina and Arbaaz. The chicken biryani was delicious; the grains of rice were so long, and each grain was cooked to perfection! The seviyan was out of this world.

Amina told me that Eid ul-Fitr is an important religious festival celebrated by Muslims. It marks the end of Ramzan or Ramadan, the Islamic holy month of fasting, in which Muslims fast from sunrise to sunset for twenty-nine or thirty days. Aziz Aunty told us that because Muslims follow the lunar calendar, which depends on the moon, the precise time of the Eid celebration varies from place to place and depends on when the religious authorities of that particular place sight the new moon.

I also asked Aziz Aunty the meaning of Fitra, as I had heard Amina talk about it. She explained that Fitra, also called Fitrana or Fitrah, is an obligatory charity that is done for the poor during the month of fasting. She said it was the monetary equivalent of 2.5 kg of wheat per head. As the Aziz household had fourteen members, it was 2.5 kg of the quality of wheat they ate, multiplied by the number of people in that household (fourteen). She told us that the Fitra was to be paid before the Eid prayer by the head of the family on behalf of each member of his family. She also said that Fitra could either be given in cash or as food.

Aziz Aunty further explained that the reason behind giving the Fitra was to ensure that everyone could celebrate Eid. She said that Ramzan was the time of the year when the Muslims put special emphasis on charity.

I enjoyed meeting Amina and Arbaaz's family. It must be nice staying in a joint family; so many people living in one house must be real fun. Amina and Arbaaz told us that their Ami would ask

Dadi to let us have a sleepover in their house sometime soon. I hope Dadi agrees.

The food was yummy — the biryani and the seviyan were the most delicious. It was sweet of Aziz Aunty to keep the gulab jamuns as a part of the Eid spread. Everyone complimented us on the sweets. Later, when I told Lata didi that her gulab jamuns were a hit, she couldn't stop smiling.

I'm all praise for Amina and Arbaaz. Both are so young, yet they kept the Roza. In fact, this was their second year keeping the fast. I also learnt three Urdu words: Shukriya, which means thanks; Mubarak, which means congratulations; and Insha Allah, which means God willing. Urdu words sound really sweet.

I forgot to mention that there was a sweet made from dates, which was just amazing.

21

Guru Purnima Quiz
with Mrs Rathore

Dadi and Sarla Aunty had been mentioning Guru Purnima so often that the twins' curiosity was piqued. 'What is this Guru Purnima?' Natasha asked.

'Guru Purnima is an Indian tradition dedicated to the spiritual teachers who, as enlightened humans, share their wisdom to make the world a better place to live in,' Sarla Aunty said.

'Oh, it sounds like teachers' day,' Nikhil said.

'Kind of,' Sarla Aunty replied. 'But these spiritual teachers or masters don't expect or get any monetary benefit from their students. Whatever they do is only from the goodness of their heart.'

'Okay,' Natasha said. 'Something like the rishis of the past?'

'Yes,' Sarla Aunty smiled. 'The word Guru is derived from two words – gu and ru. The Sanskrit root 'gu' means darkness or ignorance, and 'ru' denotes the remover of that darkness. Therefore, a Guru is one who removes the darkness of our ignorance.'

'Even our school teachers remove our ignorance of many subjects,' Nikhil grinned. 'Were it not for their immense patience and teaching, we would all be complete dumbos.'

'Yes, school teachers are also gurus,' Sarla Aunty nodded. 'On this day, disciples pay their respect to their Gurus. In addition to the religious significance, this festival is also important for students and scholars, who thank their teachers for giving them knowledge.'

'I have an idea,' Natasha whispered to Nikhil.

'It's super,' he said. 'How come you always get the better ideas?' he frowned.

'That's because most of your energy is focused on food,' she winked.

'Yeah, as if you live on air and water.'

On Guru Purnima, which was not a school holiday, Nikhil and Natasha carried a stack of cards and chocolates to school. After making all their classmates sign the cards, they stacked the cards on their desks.

Before a teacher entered their classroom, they placed a card and some chocolates on the teacher's desk. Each card said 'Happy Guru Purnima'.

'I've never received a Guru Purnima card before,' Mrs Devika Rathore, their History teacher, said with a smile.

'This is such a wonderful gesture. I'm declaring a free period today. Seeing your sweet gesture, how can I take a class today?'

'Yippee!' the students screamed.

'Give me a minute.' She walked out of the classroom, returning five minutes later with a large cardboard box.

'Let's play a game,' she said.

'Yay,' the students said.

'It's called one-word association game,' she smiled. 'I'll mention different things—it could be anything—you must tell me the first word that comes to your mind. Like, if I say sky, I'm sure you will all say blue. But you can also

say birds or airplanes as they both fly in the sky, or even the Sun, Moon and the stars. The student that gives the best answer will get a chocolate from me. The student or students with the most chocolates at the end of the game are the winners.'

'Let's start,' Arbaaz said excitedly.

'School,' Mrs Rathore said.

'Education,' Amina said.

'Teachers,' Nikhil screamed.

'Exams,' a student said, making a face.

'Uniform,' Natasha screamed.

Mrs Rathore threw a chocolate towards Natasha.

'Book,' their teacher said.

'Stories,' Amina screamed.

'Lessons,' Nikhil said.

'Writing,' Ruhi said from the second last row.

'Adventure,' Natasha said.

Their teacher threw another chocolate towards Natasha.

'Grey,' Mrs Rathore said.

'Dull,' Gaurav, who sat in the first row, said.

'Colour,' Amina yelled.

'Boring,' Arbaaz said.

'Cloud,' Natasha said.

Natasha received her third chocolate!

'Nikhil,' the teacher said, with a mischievous twinkle in her eyes.

'Boy,' Gaurav laughed.

'Clever,' Amina smiled.

'America,' Arbaaz grinned.

'Glutton,' Natasha giggled.

'Looks like Natasha is going to win this game,' Mrs Rathore said, throwing yet another chocolate towards Natasha.

'Witches,' she said.

'Scary,' Vedika, a girl in the third row said.

'Evil,' Natasha screamed.

'Wand,' Hemant laughed.

'Magic,' Nikhil said.

The chocolate landed in Nikhil's lap.

At the end of the game, Natasha was the clear winner.

Natasha's Journal

I'm glad I could show my appreciation to all my teachers on Guru Purnima. All the teachers were very happy with our gesture. I do get some amazing ideas! I hope I don't sound like Nikhil.

Sarla Aunty said Guru Purnima is celebrated by Hindus, Buddhists and Jains. It's a day to pay respects to one's chosen spiritual teachers and thank them for their guidance. Sarla Aunty also told us that this day is celebrated during a full moon, called Purnima in the Hindu month of Ashadha, which corresponds to either June or July in the Gregorian calendar.

Buddhists celebrate this day in honour of Lord Buddha, who is believed to have delivered his first sermon on this day at Sarnath in Uttar Pradesh. Many Hindus celebrate this day in honour of the sage Ved Vyasa, who, it is believed, was born on this day. Therefore, the day is also referred to as Vyasa Purnima. Ved Vyasa is considered one of the greatest Gurus and a symbol of the Guru–Shishya tradition. Sarla Aunty called it Guru Shishya Parampara, as that is the traditional name. Students of Indian classical music and dance also follow the Guru Shishya Parampara and pay tribute to their teachers on this day.

Sarla Aunty told us a very interesting story. Eklavya was a Bhil prince, who wanted to learn archery from Guru Dronacharya in his Gurukul. However, since he wasn't from a royal family, Dronacharya refused to teach him. Eklavya then decided to learn archery so that he could become the greatest archer in the world. And because he considered Dronacharya his Guru, even though he had been turned away by him, he made a mud statue of Dronacharya and worshipped it.

One day, when Dronacharya was out in the forest with his royal students, he saw a peculiar sight. A dog was unable to bark because arrows were stuck around his mouth, which left him unharmed yet unable to bark. Dronacharya looked at the dog with concern, as it struck him that there seemed to be an archer better than his student, Arjun, which in turn meant that he would not be able to fulfil his promise of making Arjun the best archer in the world.

When Dronacharya asked Eklavya who his Guru was, he replied that it was Dronacharya himself. Eklavya then asked what he could offer his Guru. Dronacharya replied that since Eklavya had called him his Guru, he would need to give him Guru Dakshina, which is something that is given to one's teacher as a mark of respect. Dronacharya asked Eklavya for his right thumb. Though Eklavya knew that he would never become a skilled archer if he gave his right thumb to Dronacharya, he did not hesitate to cut off his thumb and offer it to his Guru. Eklavya has now become a part of the Guru Purnima folklore due to his dedication to his Guru.

For me, the best part of this festival was the look of surprise and delight on our teachers' faces when they received a greeting card on Guru Purnima. They are more used to being wished on Teachers' Day!

22

Master Chef Nikhil's
Akuri for Navroz

One Saturday, Dadi decided that it was time Nikhil had his first cooking lesson. To keep it simple, she asked him to prepare breakfast for everyone that morning. Everyone brainstormed what would be the easiest, safest and fastest dish for Nikhil to make.

'Aloo paratha,' Dadu said. It was his favourite dish.

'Poha,' Natasha said.

'No way, poha is very tricky. If I soak the beaten rice for too long in water, it will become a big lump,' Nikhil said, making a face.

'Sandwiches,' Lata said.

'Too simple!' Dadi dismissed the suggestion, adding, 'I've an idea! Since today is Navroz, the Parsi New Year, let Nikhil make akuri.'

Only Dadu smiled. Lata and Natasha looked puzzled.

'Akuri is simple to make, and there is less likelihood of

Nikhil spoiling the dish.' Dadi grinned. 'Akuri is Parsi-style scrambled eggs.'

'Cool!' Nikhil grinned too. 'I love the name, and if the chef likes the name, the dish is going to rock!'

'What weird logic,' Natasha said, blowing a strand of hair from her face. 'Whatever! But please make it fast; we don't like late breakfast.'

'Can I invite Sarla Aunty and Sushil Uncle for breakfast?' Nikhil asked excitedly.

'Of course,' Dadi smiled. 'She is your favourite person in the world.'

'Lata, make mooli paratha and boondi raita as a backup, just in case something goes wrong,' Dadi said softly.

'Good idea, Madam,' Lata said. 'I'll tell Nikhil I'm making them for lunch.'

Before starting to cook, Nikhil went to the puja room to seek blessings from the gods as though he was going to the battlefront.

Dadu wrote 'Master Chef Nikhil' with a marker on a white apron and gave it to Nikhil. Just then the doorbell rang. Lata opened the door to let Sarla Aunty in. She handed Nikhil a big box of chocolates. 'Good luck, sweetheart,' she said, hugging him. 'Your uncle has gone for a snooker match, so he couldn't make it.'

Everyone followed Nikhil into the kitchen. Lata was already at work, rolling out the mooli parathas. Dadi had laid out all the ingredients on the counter. She had even printed out the easiest recipe she could find.

Nikhil started measuring out the ingredients according to the proportions listed in the recipe. First, he broke six eggs into a dish and kept it aside. Then, taking five black peppercorns, he coarsely pounded them with a pestle in a mortar. Once this was done, he washed a few cilantro leaves, popularly known as coriander leaves. Shaking them dry, he chopped them finely on the counter. Lata had given him a knife with a blunt edge to chop the cilantro.

'I've already chopped the onions for you, as it's your first time in the kitchen. I can't risk you cutting your fingers,' Dadi said.

'Thank you, Dadi,' Nikhil smiled nervously.

Next, he added the milk, salt, coarsely ground pepper and chopped cilantro into the eggs and beat them lightly with a fork.

Taking a large skillet, he added two tablespoons of butter into it. Then, switching on the gas, he placed the skillet over it. Once the butter had started to melt, he added in the finely chopped onions.

'Keep stirring so that the onions colour evenly and don't burn,' he said to the group gathered in the kitchen.

'Wonderful tip, chef Nikhil,' Sarla Aunty smiled.

While the onions were sweating, he put four slices of bread into the toaster. Once the onions had turned pink, he added the chopped chillies, red pepper, turmeric and powdered cumin. He stirred the mixture for two to three minutes. Then, he slowly poured the beaten eggs into the skillet, constantly stirring the mixture with a spatula until the eggs set.

'Don't overcook them,' he advised his audience. 'The mixture should be creamy not dry.'

By the time he switched off the gas burner, the toaster had popped out the bread. Nikhil transferred the scrambled eggs into a dish and the toasted bread onto a plate.

'You all can start eating breakfast while I toast the remaining bread,' Lata said.

Sarla Aunty spread scrambled egg over her toasted bread.

After the first bite, she said, 'Best akuri I've ever eaten.'
Nikhil beamed with pleasure.

Nikhil's Nook

Hi Friends,

*Today, I took the first step towards my dream of becoming a chef.
As it was Navroz, I decided to celebrate it by making the easiest
and the simplest version of akuri, or Parsi-style scrambled eggs.*

*Navroz is the Parsi New Year. It is spelt in different ways:
Nowruz, Navroze or Navruz. But either way, 'nav' means new and
'roz' means day, so Navroz means 'new day'.*

Parsis celebrate their new year around the third week of August.

*Navroz is the day on which Parsis symbolically cleanse their souls
and ask for forgiveness for past mistakes so that they can start the
new year afresh and pray that it brings love, hope, kindness, health,
peace and prosperity.*

*Parsis wear new clothes on the festival and clean and decorate
their homes. Sarla Aunty said they make chalk designs outside the*

main door using trays that have designs perforated in them. They make different kinds of designs. If it is that of a fish, they make the body with chalk powder and the eye of the fish with red powder. They also decorate the doorway with torans and flowers and grow wheatgrass in their homes on this occasion.

Parsis give gifts and make charitable donations on Navroz. They also greet each other on this festival, sprinkling rose water on their guests to welcome them into their home.

When I heard the names of the dishes Parsis eat on Navroz, my mouth started to water. Dadi promised to make two of these dishes for me. The dishes are called ravo and sev. Ravo is made from semolina, milk and sugar, and sev is a sweet dish made with fried vermicelli and sugar syrup and garnished with dry fruit.

All these Parsi dishes that are part of the Navroz feast sound delicious — prawn patio, mori dar, patra ni machi, chicken farcha, fried fish, saffron pulao and lagan nu custard.

Before I say goodbye, I must add that my akuri was good! Everyone enjoyed it.

23

Nikhil's Gluttony on Onam

'I don't want you to spend the entire day cooking,' Dadi told Lata. 'Onam is your festival, you should celebrate it with family and friends, instead of cooking for us.'

'Madam, you all are my family and friends,' Lata said, her voice choked with emotion. 'I still remember how you saved me after my marriage broke down and my parents refused to accept me back into my maternal home. I am so grateful that you and sir gave me a job,' she said between sobs.

'Oh no, stop it, Lata. I don't want you to cry on a festival day,' Dadi rushed to her side. Hugging her, she said, 'I'm sure if not us, someone else would have helped you.'

'You and sir have been very kind to me, sending me for cooking classes, teaching me Hindi,' Lata sobbed. 'You even gave me the option of working with someone else. I can never think of leaving this house.'

'Now go to the kitchen, Lata,' Dadi ordered. 'If you want my help, let me know. Even Sarla called to offer her assistance. Onasadya is an elaborate affair, so we would like to help you.'

Lata had prepared an Onam feast or Onasadya. The Kapoors had invited the Sadhwanis. And the twins had invited their friends, Amina and Arbaaz, Reema, Raunak, and Pema and their favourite teacher, Sharbani Basu.

'Thank you, Madam,' Lata wiped her tears, 'I've finished the cooking. I just need to make the pookalam. I bought the flowers yesterday and depetalled them. By the time everyone arrives for lunch, my pookalam will be ready.'

'I'll help you carry the flowers,' Nikhil volunteered.

'And I'll help you make the pookam,' Natasha said with a smile.

'It's pookalam, not pookam,' Lata laughed.

The twins were wearing the clothes they had worn for the Eid lunch.

'Lata, make a small pookalam outside the main door, but make a larger one in the hall where it can stay for a couple of days. The milkman, newspaperman and dhobi always spoil the one outside by stepping on it and crushing the flowers,' their grandmother grumbled.

'That's a wonderful idea!' Lata's eyes shone with pleasure. 'That way I can make two pookalams. I have enough flowers for both.'

Nikhil carried the flowers wrapped in newspaper to the living room. Natasha sat cross-legged beside Lata, watching her make the elaborate floral pattern.

'Nikhil, you can wipe the banana leaves with a wet cloth, but make sure you don't tear them,' Dadi ordered. As Nikhil went into the kitchen, she told her husband, 'That will keep him out of the way.'

It took forty-five minutes to complete the pookalam in the living room. Lata had made an elaborate sun, filling the concentric circles within it with flowers of different colours.

By the time they were done, the guests had started to trickle in. Reema and Raunak were the first to arrive. They were

dressed in traditional clothes – Reema in a peach-coloured churidar-kurta and Raunak in a grey churidar-kurta; they had brought along a steel box filled with murukkus and besan laddoos. Amina and Arbaaz entered the house a little later in their Eid outfits. They had brought a sweet made from dates and a box of chocolates. Sarla Aunty and Sushil Uncle looked perfectly matched when they entered the house a short while later, Aunty in a pink sari and uncle in a pale-pink churidar-kurta. They had brought along chikkis and doodh pak, which is a thick kheer made with rice.

Pema arrived carrying two plates covered with napkins in his hands. He had also worn a cream churidar-kurta.

He shyly offered the plates to Dadi.

'What is this, Pema?' she asked, removing the napkins that covered the two plates.

'Vegetable momos and sel roti,' he said softly.

'What is sel roti?' Dadi asked.

'It is prepared from fermented rice batter, which is deep fried in the shape of rings,' he said. 'I helped Mom make them.'

'You must teach us how to make it,' Sarla Aunty said. 'It looks delicious.'

Lata hurried to the main door with half a dozen packets of flowers. She quickly made the outline of the floral pattern.

Sharbani Ma'am was the last to arrive. She was dressed in

a light-pink salwar-kurta, her long hair in a French braid. She was carrying two boxes of sweets.

'Dadu, Dadi, Lata didi, Sushil Uncle and Sarla Aunty, this is Sharbani Ma'am, our Maths teacher,' Natasha said.

'Hello,' Sharbani Ma'am said. 'Thank you for inviting me over,' she said warmly. 'This is for you,' she handed the boxes of sweets to Dadi.

'There was no need for all this, dear,' Dadi said. 'We just want your company.'

'It's nothing, Ma'am,' their teacher said. 'Just some Bengali sweets.'

'Call me aunty,' Dadi smiled.

'I refuse to put on weight with all the food everyone has brought,' Dadi announced a few minutes later. 'After lunch, you all will help me divide everything so that you can take some part of it home. That way, the calories will be divided equally amongst all of us!'

Everyone laughed.

'Have no fear, I'm here,' Nikhil patted his stomach.

'Ma'am, can I see the mehendi on your hands?' Natasha said.

Sharbani Ma'am showed Natasha her hands. The mehendi had faded, and only a faint pattern was visible.

'It was my best friend's first Teej after her wedding; she had invited me to her house for the celebrations,' Sharbani Ma'am explained.

'Hariyali Teej, right?' Sarla Aunty asked.

'You know about the Teej festival?' Sharbani Ma'am asked.

'We lived in Jaipur for five years. I loved being part of the Teej celebrations,' Sarla Aunty explained. Turning to Nikhil, she said, 'You will love the sweets that are made for Teej. Remind me to make ghevar for you.'

'I'll remind you tomorrow itself,' Nikhil grinned.

'Can I help with the pookalam?' Sharbani ma'am turned to Lata.

'That will be lovely!' Lata looked happy. 'I'm doing the outline. You can fill it in with the leftover flowers, while I heat the food.'

Sharbani Ma'am sat down beside Natasha. Amina and Reema also joined them. They all quickly filled the pattern with flower petals of different colours. Sharbani Ma'am did most of the work. She had a clean hand; the circle she had filled was so neat that it looked as though it had been painted.

'This is beautiful!' Lata exclaimed when she came there a few minutes later to check the progress. 'You are doing a wonderful job, have you done this before?'

'Yes, once in school, for a competition,' Sharbani Ma'am said.

'I am sorry you are all having to work,' Lata said.

'No, no, it's my pleasure. I love doing this,' she replied.

Fifteen minutes later, the floral arrangement was complete.

Lata announced that lunch was ready. It was decided that the children and Sharbani Ma'am would eat first as the dining table could seat only eight people at a time.

Lata had laid out eight banana leaves. One by one, she served the dishes, telling the children the name and the ingredients of each dish: lemon pickle, mango pickle, banana chips, papadam, pachadi, white rice, aviyal, sambar, rasam, curd, buttermilk, dal, thoran, a white pumpkin curry made in coconut milk, yam and drumstick, two types of payasam and a small banana.

'Oh my God,' Nikhil said. 'This is a feast fit for the gods.'

'I've never eaten anything so delicious,' Arbaaz sighed. 'This is heaven on a leaf.'

'I'm in a food coma,' Amina said.

'It's delicious,' Pema said.

'I'm not saying anything,' Reema said. 'These four have stolen my words.'

'I'm planning to eat second helpings of everything,' Nikhil announced. 'Be warned, Lata didi, you may run out of food.'

'No worries dear, I've made lots.' Lata ruffled his hair.

The children ate well, taking generous second helpings. Finally, they folded their banana leaves, signifying the end of their feast.

Having stuffed himself, Nikhil could barely stand up. Trudging to the sofa, he plonked down on it.

Suma, their other house help, cleared the table and set fresh leaves for the remaining people. For a plump person, Suma was very agile. She dressed in silk saris, and the flowers in her hair fell all over the house while she did the sweeping and swabbing.

'Lata, you eat. Let Suma serve us,' Dadi said.

The adults finished much sooner than the children.

'Lata, you must give me the recipe for this aviyal and payasam,' Sarla Aunty said. 'Both are out of this world.'

After the adults had finished eating, Dadi and Sarla Aunty insisted that Lata take it easy now that the meal was over. With Suma's help, they cleared up everything and divided the food that everyone had brought with them into small disposable containers for each of them to take back home.

By late afternoon, the guests started to leave. Each one was handed a goodie box by Dadi.

Nikhil sat on the sofa, groaning with discomfort. By evening, he had a terrible stomach ache.

He rolled on his bed, clutching his stomach. A worried Lata sat beside him, holding his hand, while Dadi called the family doctor.

The doctor arrived an hour later.

After examining Nikhil, the doctor said it was a case of indigestion. 'Light food for the next few days, preferably idlis for breakfast, khichdi or curd rice for lunch and boiled vegetables and homemade soup for dinner. No heavy food for a week.'

As per the doctor's instruction, Nikhil was given the prescribed diet.

'I've lost two kilos,' he announced at breakfast a few days later. 'Never again will I indulge in gluttony,' he said with a shudder.

Natasha's Journal

Our Onasadya was a huge hit. Everyone praised the dishes and showered Lata didi with compliments. The entire day, Lata didi was floating on a cloud of happiness. This will also be a memorable Onam for Nikhil. His gluttony got him into trouble. And the doctor's diet made him lose weight. I think he will never overeat again in his life. But with Nikhil, you never know.

Dadi smartly divided all the food everyone had brought, so that all our guests had something to take back home. She is so generous and clever!

Lata didi told me the significance of Onam. It is an annual festival of Kerala and falls in the month of August or September in the Gregorian calendar. Onam is a harvest festival and celebrates the homecoming of King Mahabali. Lata didi said Onam celebrations last for ten days and include tug of war competitions, snake boat races, flower arrangement competitions and different kinds of dances such as Kummattikali, a mask dance in which dancers wearing different kinds of wooden masks go from house to house entertaining people and collecting gifts from them; and the Pulikkali dance, in which dancers paint their bodies to appear like tigers and wear tiger masks. It all sounded so amazing that I made Lata didi promise to take me to Kerala for next year's Onam celebrations.

Lata didi also narrated an interesting story behind Onam. According to Hindu mythology, Mahabali—the great grandson of the demonic ruler Hiranyakashyap and the grandson of Prahalad, the devotee of Vishnu—defeated the gods and became the ruler of the three worlds. When the defeated gods appealed to Lord Vishnu for help, he refused to help them as Mahabali was a good and kind ruler, despite being an Asura king. After his victory over the gods, Mahabali organized a yajna. During the yajna, he declared that he would grant people's wishes. It is believed that Vishnu decided to test Mahabali's devotion and also vanquish the ego he had developed, so he assumed the avatar of a dwarf called Vamana and approached Mahabali. Mahabali offered the dwarf boy gold, precious stones, land, food, cows, elephants and anything that he desired. But the boy said that he wanted a piece of land that measured 'three paces'. Thinking that this short boy wouldn't be able to cover much ground, Mahabali agreed. However, the Vamana started to grow in height and soon covered everything Mahabali ruled over in just two strides. When he saw this, Mahabali realized that this was no mere mortal and must be a god in disguise, who had come to test him. Before the Vamana could take the third step, Mahabali bent his head and offered himself, requesting that the Vamana place his foot over his head. Vishnu accepted this request as a sign of Mahabali's devotion and humility and placed his foot over his bowed head. He then pressed on his bowed head and sent him into the netherworld. Pleased with Mahabali's devotion and sincerity in keeping his promise, Vishnu granted him a boon and assured him that he could visit the lands and the people he had ruled once a year. Onam symbolizes Mahabali's annual visit to Earth. The last day of his visit is celebrated with an elaborate vegetarian feast called Onasadya, which Lata didi had prepared for us.

Sharbani Ma'am told us that she enjoyed the Hariyali Teej celebrations. She enjoyed keeping the fast, dressing up in a red-and-green salwar-kurta and applying mehendi on her hands. She said that Hariyali Teej is also called Choti Teej or Shravan Teej and is celebrated during the monsoon season in Rajasthan, Bihar, Uttar Pradesh, Madhya Pradesh and Haryana. She said Hariyali Teej is dedicated to Goddess Parvati and Lord Shiva, and is celebrated in July or August in the Gregorian calendar. Sharbani Ma'am told us she and her friends kept a day-long fast without even a sip of water and broke the fast in the evening after praying to Lord Shiva and Goddess Parvati and the moon. All the food she mentioned—ghevar, kheer, jalebi, malpua, puri, paneer and halwa—made Nikhil's mouth water. I'm sure he will bug Sarla Aunty to make ghevar for him tomorrow.

24

Raksha Bandhan
Surprise for Natasha

Nikhil was being very secretive, spending most of his time on the phone or on his laptop. Whenever Natasha entered the room, he would either close his laptop or slip into the balcony if he was on the phone. She knew he was planning something that he didn't want to share with her. Natasha was disappointed. They had never kept anything from each other. The only thing she had hidden from him was Sushil Uncle's story about his efforts to be a superhero, but that was a promise she had made to uncle and promises weren't meant to be broken.

Her eyes brimming with tears, she walked out of his room. She had decided she wouldn't ask him anything. If he wanted to hide things from her, she was fine with it.

As Raksha Bandhan was around the corner, Lata took Natasha shopping after school. Muniraju dropped them near the street that was lined with shops on both sides.

'Don't wait,' Lata told the driver. 'We will come back on our own.'

Every shop was crowded with last-minute shoppers.

After walking a short distance, they stopped at a stall that was selling rakhis. There were rakhis of all shapes and sizes, with beads, feathers and ribbons.

'Choose your rakhi,' Lata said.

Natasha chose a medium-sized red rakhi with gold beads in the centre. She checked the thread to make sure it wouldn't snap easily.

'How much?' Lata asked the shopkeeper.

'Fifty rupees,' he replied, tucking the rakhi into a brown envelope.

Natasha paid the amount and, taking the packet from the shopkeeper's hands, carefully tucked it into her red handbag.

'Don't worry, it won't break,' Lata laughed. Lata also chose a small rakhi for herself.

'This is for twenty rupees,' the stall owner said.

'Please pack it for me,' Lata said, giving the man the exact change.

'For your brother?' Natasha asked.

'I don't have a brother. In fact, we Malayalis don't celebrate rakhi, but after I started working with madam and sir, I fell in love with this ritual of Raksha Bandhan,' she smiled. 'I decided I'll tie my rakhi to Lord Krishna.'

'You have a powerful brother,' Natasha smiled. 'Why did you buy such a small and thin rakhi?'

'My brother has a tiny wrist compared to your brother.' Lata's eyes twinkled with mischief.

'Your brother is not a glutton like mine,' Natasha giggled. Both laughed.

'You wanted to buy a gift and sweets for Nikhil, right?' Lata asked.

They had stopped outside a sweet shop. It was packed with customers. They joined the throng of people inside the small shop.

There was a mind-boggling variety of sweets on display — barfi, laddoo, peda, soan papdi, kaju katli, sandesh, rasgulla, gulab jamun and halwa.

'Nikhil would have wanted to sample everything,' Natasha laughed. She bought half a kilo of kesar malai pedas, which were Nikhil's perennial favourite, and a box of truffle chocolates. Lata bought sandesh for Lord Krishna.

'Anything else?' asked the man at the counter, as he weighed their sweets in colourful cardboard boxes. Tying the boxes with gold ribbons, he gave them the bill to pay at the cash counter.

After they had paid and collected their sweets and box of chocolates, Lata bought two ice creams from a small shop. They strolled down the street eating their ice creams.

'I wonder what Nikhil is going to gift me for Raksha Bandhan?' Natasha frowned. 'Usually, Mom picks up the gift on his behalf. Last year he had asked me what I wanted. But this year, he has been silent.'

'No idea, dear,' Lata said. 'You will come to know tomorrow what he has bought for you.'

'I hope he hasn't forgotten.'

They reached the end of the street.

'You enjoy travelling in auto rickshaws, so we will go home in one.' Lata hailed an auto.

'I hate it when festivals fall on Saturdays and Sundays. That way we don't get extra holidays,' Natasha said, as the auto trundled over the roads.

On Raksha Bandhan, Natasha rose early. She wore the yellow bandhani kurta that Lata had given her on Vishu, over the crinkled white skirt that had been gifted to her by Sarla Aunty.

Dadi arranged the aarti thali for her: a few grains of rice, saffron soaked in water for the tilak, flower petals, two sweets and a silver diya with a wick soaked in ghee.

'Be careful,' her grandmother said, lighting the cotton wick.

Nikhil emerged from his room. He wore the blue embossed kurta that Lata had gifted him over blue denims.

'Same pinch!' He pinched his sister's arm.

As instructed by her grandmother, Natasha did the aarti for her brother, then applied the saffron tilak on his forehead and another tilak of rice grains, which stuck to his forehead due to the watery saffron paste. Showering him with rose petals, she tied the rakhi on his right wrist. She then offered him the sweet.

Instead of taking a bite of the peda, Nikhil opened his mouth wide and swallowed the entire sweet. His cheeks bulged as he ate the peda.

'You are supposed to make her eat the sweet too,' Dadi said and shook her head.

'Oops,' he said. Taking the second sweet from the thali, he offered it to his sister.

Natasha handed him the box of chocolates and pedas.

'Super,' he said. 'But I didn't get any gift for you,' he said, showing her his empty hands.

'You told me that you have picked up your sister's gift.' Dadi frowned.

'Don't worry, Dadi, I've got it all under control,' he smiled. 'Natasha wanted to learn Bharatnatyam, so I've organized two months of classes for her with Sharbani Ma'am's guruji. Her classes will be twice a week. She can choose the days.'

'That's awesome!' Natasha hugged her brother.

'What a thoughtful gift,' Dadi said, wiping the tears from her eyes with the edge of her green dupatta.

Bending down, Nikhil lifted a gift-wrapped box from underneath the sofa. 'Here are the ghungroos,' he said, handing her the box. 'Happy Raksha Bandhan, Sis.'

'You bought the ghungroos for me?' Natasha asked.

'Nope, Sharbani Ma'am did, but I paid for them. But the idea of the dance classes was mine,' he said. 'In two months, you will come to know whether you like the dance and want to continue the classes.'

Nikhil's Nook

Hi Friends,

When I told my sister that I hadn't bought any Rakhi gift for her, her face fell. But when I told her about the dance classes I had arranged for her, she was super excited. And she just couldn't stop playing with the ghungroos.

Raksha Bandhan is also called Rakhi. It is a festival in which sisters tie a thread, or a rakhi, on the wrist of their brothers. This thread is a symbol of the sister's love and affection for her brother. In return, brothers give their sisters a gift and promise to protect their sisters all their lives. The thread that the sisters tie on their brothers' wrist can be an amulet or a talisman – anything that is symbolic of a sister's love.

Raksha Bandhan typically falls in the month of August in the Gregorian calendar.

Dadu explained to me the symbolism of Rakhi, saying that it signifies giving a brother a share of the responsibility of looking after his sister's welfare. The thread binds the brother to his sister for life.

Sushil Uncle told us many interesting stories related to Rakhi. He said that the ritual of Rakhi dates back thousands of years.

According to the story from the Srimad Bhagavata Purana and the Vishnu Purana, after Lord Vishnu won the three worlds from Mahabali, the Asura king, and sent him to the netherworld, he decided to reward him for his devotion by protecting him. He then disguised himself as Mahabali's doorman. But Lord Vishnu's wife, Goddess Lakshmi, was not pleased and wanted Vishnu to return to their abode, Vaikuntha. So, she tied a rakhi on Mahabali's wrist and made him her brother. As a brother is supposed to give his sister a gift in return, Mahabali asked Goddess Lakshmi what gift she wanted. She replied that Mahabali should free Vishnu from his promise of staying with him. Mahabali couldn't refuse and had to allow the gods to return to Vaikuntha.

This wasn't the only story Sushil Uncle told us. He said that a myth attributes the festival of Raksha Bandhan to Lord Yama or the Lord of Death and his sister, the Yamuna River. It is believed that once Yamuna tied a sacred thread on Yama's wrist. Yama was so pleased with his sister that he blessed her with immortality. He also said that brothers who get rakhis tied on their wrists by their sisters and promise to protect them will be blessed with immortality. Yet another story dates back to the Mahabharata. Once, Lord Krishna cut his little finger and it started to bleed. Draupadi tore a piece of her sari and tied it on Krishna's finger to stop the bleeding. Lord Krishna promised to repay this debt whenever Draupadi needed his help in the future.

I'll also protect Natasha all my life.

25

Natasha's Shrikhand
for Janmashtami

'Dadi, I want to try my hand at cooking too,' Natasha said at breakfast. 'Could you please suggest some easy recipe I can try today?'

'Copycat!' Nikhil made a face.

'Hmm, let me think,' Dadi said. 'Today is Janmashtami. Why don't you make shrikhand?'

'That sounds so complicated,' Natasha said, looking wide-eyed at her grandmother.

'No, no, I'll teach you Sarla's recipe. It's so simple and easy that even a child can make it.' Dadi pursed her lips. 'In fact, we will ask Sarla to teach you. I'll find out if she is free today.' Dadi lifted the intercom and dialled Sarla Aunty's number.

'Sarla, Natasha wants to learn how to make shrikhand. Are you free to teach her?' Dadi asked. 'Oh good, I'll keep it all ready. See you after lunch.'

Dadi kept the receiver down. 'She has asked me to keep some hung curd ready,' she said. 'Let's do that now, so that by afternoon, it's all ready for her to teach you.'

'I'll also join you all,' Nikhil said.

They followed Dadi into the kitchen.

'Pour this dish of fresh curd into the centre of a muslin cloth,' Dadi instructed Natasha.

'Won't it leak out?' Natasha asked. Her grandmother shook her head. Natasha poured the entire curd into the muslin cloth.

'Now, gather the ends and twist it into a knot, so there is a lump at the centre,' Dadi instructed.

Natasha gathered the four ends of the cloth, and as she held it up, the curd collected in the middle of the thin white cloth.

'I'll do this part for you,' Dadi said, taking the cloth from her. 'By doing this, I'm draining out all the excess water from the curd. This water is called the whey.' After tying the knot, so that all the curd was trapped in the centre, she hung the cloth on the railing of the window, to let all the excess water drain into the sink. 'By the time

Sarla comes, we will have hung curd ready to turn into delicious shrikhand.'

Late in the afternoon, Sarla Aunty dropped in at the Kapoor house. Hugging the twins and their grandmother, she asked, 'Is the hung curd ready?'

'Yes,' Dadi said, leading them to the kitchen.

'Open the muslin cloth and transfer the hung curd into a cup,' Sarla Aunty instructed.

Natasha transferred the contents of the cloth into a big cup. It was a little more than a cup.

'Now powder five tablespoons of sugar in a mixer-grinder,' she instructed.

Measuring five tablespoons of sugar, Natasha carefully put it into the mixer.

'Make sure it's a fine powder; that way it will mix well in the curd,' Sarla Aunty instructed.

Soon the sound of the whirling blades of the mixer filled the kitchen. A few minutes later, Natasha had her powdered sugar mix ready.

'Add it into the bowl of hung curd along with a few strands of kesar. It will give it a lovely yellow colour,' she said.

Natasha added three strands of kesar and the entire sugar into the bowl.

'Now beat well with a spoon, until all the sugar blends into the hung curd. Hung curd tends to be a little sour, so we have to add a good amount of sugar,' she said.

Holding the dish in her left hand, she mixed the contents with a long spoon. 'My hands are hurting,' Natasha said, after stirring for a while.

'Here, let me help you,' Nikhil volunteered.

Natasha held out the bowl to her brother. Within minutes, the creamy curd took on a light yellow colour.

'Delicious shrikhand is ready,' he said.

Lata transferred the shrikhand into a small silver bowl. They all trooped into the puja room. Dadi and Lata had adorned the idol of Lord Krishna with colourful clothes and necklaces. There was also a small mukut (crown) on his head.

Natasha placed the bowl at the feet of Lord Krishna. As instructed by Lata, she covered the bowl with a banana leaf.

Natasha's Journal

Like Nikhil, I too have become very attached to Sarla Aunty, and it's not because of all the yummy food she sends us. She is a sweet lady, always ready to help everyone. Today, I made shrikhand with her help. The recipe is so easy. When I sent Mom the picture of the shrikhand, Mom was both shocked and surprised. She asked if I had developed an interest in cooking like Nikhil. She also told me to make it for her when she comes to India.

Dadi kept my shrikhand as prasad for Lord Krishna as it's his birthday. Janmashtami or Gokulashtami is the day the eighth avatar of Vishnu, Krishna, is believed to have been born. Janmashtami is celebrated in the month of August or September of the Gregorian calendar.

Sarla Aunty narrated the story of Krishna's birth. Krishna was the son of Devaki and Vasudeva and was born in Mathura at midnight on the eighth day of the month of Shravana. He was born in turbulent times, when evil existed everywhere and people were denied the freedom to live the way they wanted to.

There was a threat to Krishna's life from his uncle King Kamsa, who was the ruler of the Vrishni kingdom with its capital at Mathura. Owing to a heavenly prophecy that Devaki's eighth son would slay him, Kamsa imprisoned Devaki and Vasudeva and killed all their children. When Devaki's eighth son was born, Vasudeva took the baby Krishna across the Yamuna to Gokul. He left Krishna at the home of Nanda, the head of cowherds, and Yashoda, so he could be brought up by his foster parents. Kamsa sent many demons to kill little Krishna, all of whom were killed by him. Finally, Krishna ended Kamsa's reign by slaying him in Mathura and freeing the people of his kingdom from his cruel rule.

Sarla Aunty said that on Janmashtami, people fast and sing devotional songs for Krishna. They wait for midnight to celebrate his birth, after which statues of baby Krishna are dressed in new clothes and placed in cradles. Some women draw tiny footprints outside the main entrance of the house to signify a baby walking into the house. This is symbolic of Krishna's journey into their homes.

Sarla Aunty also told me that Lord Krishna loved eating butter, and when he was a small child, he would not only have butter from his house but also take it from the houses of other people. His mother would tie the butter pot near the ceiling so that he couldn't reach it. One day, while his mother was out of the house, Krishna gathered all his friends and made a human pyramid to reach the pot by climbing everyone's shoulders. He then enjoyed the butter along with his friends.

I loved hearing Krishna's childhood stories and about his love for butter. I do hope Krishna enjoyed the shrikhand I offered him!

26

Dadi's Ganesh Chaturthi Tales

'Dadi, you promised to tell me the story of the various idols of gods in your puja room,' Natasha said as she sat reading a book in the living room with her grandmother and Nikhil.

Dadi was doing her crochet—a pink border for her friend Sarla—and Nikhil was watching the Ganesh Chaturthi processions on T.V.

'I'll tell you how I started worshipping Ganesha or Ganpati Bappa,' Dadi said. 'When I was your age, I had failed in my school tests in two subjects: Maths and Chemistry. After our class teacher distributed our corrected test papers, she asked us to get our parents' signature on them. I was petrified of my father's reaction. The only saving grace was that it was a Friday, so I had the entire weekend to think of something.'

'Oh no,' Nikhil said, 'then what did you do?'

'I used to walk home with my friend and classmate, who was a Maharashtrian,' Dadi replied. 'Her name was Indu. She had failed the same tests, but while I had failed by one mark, she had failed by five.'

'What did the two of you do?' Natasha asked.

'Indu and I would walk to school and back. As we passed the Ganpati temple on the way home, we would offer our pranams,' Dadi said. 'That day, Indu was in tears. She told me her father would be very annoyed; I was scared of telling my parents too. So, when we reached the temple, instead of walking past it, as we usually did, Indu climbed the steps of the temple. She told me that she would pray to Ganpati Bappa, and request him for his help. She assured me that she would pray for me too.'

'So you didn't enter the temple?' Nikhil asked.

'Initially, I stood outside the temple. But then it struck me that since Indu was crying so much, she might forget to ask Ganpati Bappa to help me,' Dadi laughed. 'I rushed into the temple to make my own request to Ganpati Bappa.'

'We stood inside the sanctum sanctorum for some time.'

'That must have been the first time you entered a temple, right?' Natasha asked.

'Yes,' Dadi said. 'We prayed to Ganpati Bappa sincerely, to spare us our parents' temper. We also promised him that we would study hard from then on. Indu whispered to me that she had made a mannat – a vow, that she would come the next day to thank Ganpati Bappa if she was spared her father's temper. I made the same mannat.'

'Then you went home?' Natasha asked.

'Yes, when I reached home my father was having tea. I showed him my report card,' Dadi said.

'Then?' the twins asked in unison, their eyes wide open, as though they were listening to a scary story.

'Surprisingly, my father didn't get angry. He signed the answer sheets, saying, "I'll forgive you this time, but I won't be so lenient next time."' Their grandmother had a faraway look in her eyes, as she revisited these old memories.

'Indu came home after dinner and excitedly narrated to me that her father had the same reaction. So, as per our mannat, we visited the temple again the next day, which happened to be Ganesh Chaturthi, and thanked Ganpati Bappa,' Dadi said. 'We promised him that we would study hard. Ganpati Bappa has caught hold of me ever since and never let me go.' She smiled. 'All religions teach the same thing. Different religions are just different paths to the same destination. It's not important which religion one follows, what is important is that we have compassion for our fellow humans, that we help those in need, and that we show kindness in thought, words, action and speech.'

Nikhil's Nook

Hi Friends,

My grandmother's story of how Ganesha saved her from her parents' anger was adorable.

Ganesh Chaturthi, also known as Vinayaka Chaturthi or Vinayaka Chavithi, is a ten-day festival that reveres Lord Ganesha and falls in the month of August or September of the Gregorian calendar.

People install clay idols on the first day of the festival in homes or publicly in elaborate pandals. Aarti is performed every day for the duration of the festival and prasad distributed among people. The modak or laddoo is considered the favourite sweet of the elephant-headed deity. On the tenth day, the idol is carried in a public procession with music, singing and dancing, and is immersed in a body of water nearby such as a pond, lake, river or the sea.

The festival celebrates Lord Ganesha as the god of wisdom and intelligence, new beginnings and the remover of obstacles.

My entire knowledge of Ganesha comes from Sarla Aunty. Ganesha is the son of Lord Shiva and Goddess Parvati. The most popular story of his birth is from the Shiva Purana. According to this story, one day, Goddess Parvati was preparing for her bath, and to make sure that she wasn't disturbed, she made the shape of a boy from the turmeric and sandalwood paste that she was going to apply on her body. Then, she breathed life into the boy and instructed him to guard the door and not let anyone in. When Shiva emerged from his meditation and wanted to see Parvati, the small boy stopped him. Despite his proclamation that he was Parvati's husband, the boy did not let him in. Shiva then severed the boy's head with his trishul in anger. When Parvati saw what Shiva had done, she was furious and decided to destroy all of creation. Yoginis emerged from her body, threatening to destroy everything. Seeing this, Lord Brahma, the creator of the universe, was alarmed and pleaded with her to change her mind.

Parvati relented but on two conditions — that the boy be brought back to life and that he be worshipped before all the other gods.

Shiva immediately agreed to both her conditions and sent his Shiva-dutas with orders to bring back the head of the first creature they found lying dead with its head facing North. The dutas soon returned with the head of an elephant, or Gajasura. Lord Brahma then placed the head onto the boy's shoulders. The gods breathed new *life into the boy. He was given the status of being foremost among all the gods and was also declared the remover of all obstacles.*

Later, when Sushil Uncle joined us, he narrated many stories of Ganesha.

I will try to find a book that tells me more stories of this endearing god. And the modaks Sushil Uncle bought for us were delicious.

27

Durga Puja and Dandiya on Navratri

It was the weekend. The twins were playing a game of Monopoly in the living room with Pema, Reema and Raunak, while Dadi was doing her crochet and Lata was reading a book in her room.

The doorbell rang.

Lata came out of her room to open the door. Sharbani Ma'am stood outside with two mithai boxes in her hands.

'Why can't you come without all this?' Dadi asked.

'My mother sent these sweets from Kolkata. I'm sure you all will love them. Why should I put on weight alone?' Sharbani Ma'am said with a smile. 'Someone told me that we should share the calories equally.'

Everyone laughed.

'Did you get a roommate?' Dadi asked.

'Yes, my college friend who was staying as a paying guest has become my flatmate.'

'That's lovely,' their grandmother said.

'Aunty, can I take the twins to the Durga Pandal and then for Dandiya?' Sharbani Ma'am asked.

'Sure,' Dadi smiled.

'I've never seen a Durga Pandal,' Natasha said excitedly.

'And I've never done the Dandiya,' Nikhil exclaimed.

'Can we also join you?' Reema asked.

'Sure,' their teacher replied. 'My flatmate, Hetal, has an SUV. I'm sure we all can fit in.' She smiled.

At six that evening, Natasha, Nikhil, Pema, Reema and Raunak stood outside their building complex. The two girls were in ghaghra cholis, while the three boys were dressed in churidar-kurtas.

A black SUV stopped outside their building.

'You are right on time,' Sharbani Ma'am smiled. 'Children, meet my friend, Hetal Shah,' she said. 'You can call her Hetal didi.'

As the children trooped into the car, she called out their names.

'I've heard so much about you all,' Hetal didi turned around in the driver's seat. She had an oval-shaped face with high cheekbones, deep-set eyes and shoulder-length black hair. She wore a heart-shaped nose ring and dangling earrings.

They all squeezed into the back seats.

'We are super excited for both the pandal visit as well as

the Dandiya,' Raunak said. 'I once went with my friends to a dandiya event. It was fun.'

Nikhil was a little apprehensive about doing the Dandiya as he had never done it before, but Hetal didi assured him that it would be fine.

'It's easy,' Hetal didi said. 'You will soon get the hang of it.'

There was a lot of traffic on the roads, but Hetal didi was an expert driver. She weaved in and out of the chaotic traffic with ease. Finally, she stopped the vehicle outside a large ground. While she parked her SUV, they all trooped out.

They waited at the entrance for her to join them. As they stepped into the ground, they stared open-mouthed at the sight before them. The pandal was designed like a grand palace. Painted a dark gold, it glowed under the lights.

Outside, in the arena, mouth-watering aromas drifted from the food stalls.

'Stick close to each other so none of us get lost,' Sharbani Ma'am said.

They strolled into the palace, brushing past the people exiting the pandal. In the centre was a towering idol of Durga, holding different weapons in her hands. Sharbani Ma'am joined her palms in reverence, closing her eyes as she offered a prayer to the goddess. They all did the same.

After they came out of the pandal, Sharbani Ma'am said, 'Let's eat something.'

They headed towards the food stalls. There was a lip-smacking array of food: puchkas, jhaal muri, egg rolls, chicken rolls, paneer rolls, aloo kabli, singara, kachoris, mishti doi, kulfis and ice cream.

Nikhil's mouth watered.

Everyone stuffed themselves with chaat items, then washed it all down with ice cream.

After they had finished eating, they returned to the SUV. Hetal didi drove to the hall where the Dandiya night was being held. As they approached the hall, they were greeted by loud music drifting out of the hall.

The hall was as crowded as the pandal. Hetal didi picked up Dandiya sticks for all of them.

'We will show you how the Dandiya is done,' she said,

demonstrating a step with her friend.

'It doesn't look easy!' Nikhil frowned.

Beside him, Pema gulped.

'You will soon get the hang of it.' Hetal didi caught hold of Pema's arm. 'You dance with me.'

Sharbani Ma'am partnered Nikhil.

'I'll teach you,' Raunak said, turning to Nikita.

Reema teamed up with a boy her age.

A song with a fast-paced catchy beat started playing. There was a clatter of dandiya sticks as people moved around in circles, striking their sticks with those of their partner.

'This is fun,' Nikhil said a little later. He had got the hang of it quickly.

Natasha's Journal

It was sweet of Sharbani Ma'am to take us to the Durga Pandal. The pandal was gorgeous. The statue of Ma Durga was so beautiful that I could not take my eyes off it. Sharbani Ma'am treated all of us to yummy snacks. Though my jhaal muri was spicy, I still finished most of it. Nikhil gorged himself on the spicy street food. I hope he doesn't suffer from another bout of indigestion. And the rose ice cream was delicious.

Navratri, also spelled as Navaratri or Navarathri, literally means nine nights and is a Hindu festival that is celebrated differently in various parts of India. It typically falls in the months of September or October in the Gregorian calendar. Sushil Uncle explained that the nine days of Navratri are dedicated to the nine avatars of Goddess Durga: Shailaputri, Brahmcharini, Chandraghanta, Kushmunda, Skandmata, Katyayani, Kalratri, Mahagauri and Sidhidatri.

In the eastern and northeastern states of India, and most predominantly in West Bengal, Navratri is celebrated as Durga Puja. Goddess Durga is believed to have fought with and defeated the buffalo demon Mahishasura and restored righteousness and peace. In the northern and western states, the festival is synonymous with the Ramlila and Dussehra, which celebrates the victory of good over evil, symbolized by the defeat of Ravana at the hands of Lord Rama.

Today, Durga Puja is held in large, elaborately designed pandals. On Vijayadashami, the final day of Durga Puja, the Durga statues are immersed in water bodies such as ponds, lakes, rivers or the sea.

Hetal didi told us that Dandiya or Dandiya Raas is the

traditional folk dance of Gujarat and is the main dance of the Navratri festival. It originated as the devotional Garba dances, which were performed in honour of Durga. Interestingly, this dance form, called 'The Sword Dance' depicts a mock fight between Goddess Durga and Mahishasura. Dancers move around in circles performing complicated dance movements to the sound of drums. The dandiyas represent the sword of Durga. Women wear traditional dresses, such as colourful embroidered or bandhani or mirror-work ghagra-cholis and dupattas, along with jewellery. The men wear special turbans and kediyu (shirt) and kafni pyjamas.

We were all nervous about the Dandiya and very self-conscious too. But Hetal didi helped all of us practise. It was quite funny how Pema knocked the dandiya stick out of Hetal didi's hand twice! She wanted to laugh, but to avoid hurting Pema's feelings, she kept a straight face. She is as sweet as her friend. To be honest, no one was watching us as everyone was busy enjoying themselves.

28

Community Ayudha Puja

'I can't carry all my stuff,' Natasha struggled with her stack of textbooks, which she constantly adjusted in her arms. 'Could you carry my laptop and pencils, Sarla Aunty?' she asked.

'I'll carry your pens and pencils, let your Uncle hold your laptop,' Sarla Aunty said, transferring her books to her right hand and holding Natasha's pencils in her left.

Sushil Uncle carried his two snooker cues as well as Natasha's laptop.

Lata's arms were filled with an assortment of spatulas and ladles.

Nikhil held a few textbooks and his laptop in his arms.

Slowly, the group wound their way down the stairs, trying not to miss a step.

'Your Dadi comes up with the weirdest ideas,' Dadu grumbled, lugging his heavy golf bag. 'Why can't we do the Ayudha Puja in our own houses? What is the need for this community puja? By the time I carry my golf bag down these three flights of steps, I'll be nursing a tennis elbow.'

'I heard everything, Vinod,' Dadi said. 'You should have waited for the elevator, instead of acting like a young man and carrying your heavy stuff.'

'The lift was taking too damn long,' he said.

'No swearing around the children,' she warned.

On the second floor, they were joined by residents of that floor. Each one emerged from their house loaded with an array of objects. Ravi Mishra, the fifteen-year-old boy who was the captain of his school's cricket team, held his bat and textbooks in his hand. His sister, Renuka, though two years younger than him, was a couple of inches taller and carried her makeup kit.

'Hello, Aunty,' Renuka greeted Dadi.

'Hello, Renuka,' Dadi said. 'Why are you carrying your makeup kit?'

'Because I want to become a model,' she replied.

'It looks like everyone is shifting house,' Dadu grumbled.

'Why didn't you carry just one golf club?' his wife asked.

'I never know which club will help me play the winning shot,' he replied.

'Exactly,' Dadi said. 'The same rule applies to everyone.'

Pema joined them on the first floor. So high was his pile of books that only the top of his head was visible.

'Here, let me help you,' Dadi said, as she removed a few books from the large pile so that his face could be seen.

'Thank you, Aunty,' Pema looked relieved.

All the people living in the building had gathered together on the ground floor, in front of the building manager's office. Everyone clutched objects dear to them in their hands. Raunak carried his Maths and Geography textbooks and his laptop, while Reema carried her Chemistry, Biology and Algebra textbooks as well as her iPad.

The drivers had lined their cars on one side. The other building staff stood with their tools in their hands. Plumber Raju held his bag of plumbing tools. Electrician Kuppu carried his green bag of electrical tools. The three security guards stood stiffly beside the sweeping staff. All the housekeepers were dressed in traditional clothes.

A priest had been hired for the occasion. The door to the manager's office was decorated with a garland of flowers and mango leaves. Outside the office, two halves of a pumpkin, dabbed with kumkum, lay on either side of the door. Early that morning, Dadi had supervised the cleaning of the manager's office. Once everyone had deposited their stuff, there was a mountain of objects in the room.

The priest—a podgy man in a white dhoti-kurta—arranged a basket of fruit, flowers and coconuts beside all the objects.

'I hope he doesn't break a coconut over my laptop,' Nikhil whispered. Raunak laughed, inviting a sharp look from Dadi.

'What is this?' The priest held up Dadu's golf club. 'I've

never seen this before,' he inspected it carefully. 'What is it used for?'

'To cut grass,' Dadi laughed. Seeing her husband's scowl, she quickly explained, 'It's my husband's golf club. Last year, I had performed Ayudha Puja on a few of them, and he won the tournament, so this year he brought the entire lot,' she said.

'And what is this?' He held up Sushil Uncle's snooker cue.

'Same story, but a different game.' Sarla Aunty laughed. 'He also won some matches after last year's Ayudha Puja of his snooker cue!'

Sushil Uncle's face turned red.

Lighting a few agarbattis, the priest waved them around the objects. Then he sprinkled holy water over everything. With his fourth finger, he dabbed a paste of sandalwood, haldi and kumkum on the instruments and the kitchen tools. He completed the puja by showering flower petals on all the textbooks.

'Thank God, my laptop is spared,' Nikhil sighed with relief.

The priest performed the puja for each vehicle. Once again, he waved the agarbattis with his right hand and rang the brass bell with his left, chanting the mantras as he moved along. After he had applied the three finger tilak on each vehicle, he put a small garland of flowers over it.

Everyone moved to the buffet table, where Dadi had organized brunch with her prize money: upma, idli-sambar, vadas, kesari bhath and coffee.

'This is the best Ayudha Puja I've ever celebrated,' Sarla Aunty said. 'The idea of a community puja is brilliant.'

Nikhil's Nook

Hi Friends,

Today I did Ayudha Puja for the first time in my life. And I enjoyed the ritual very much. Sushil Uncle told me that Ayudha Puja is also called 'Astra Puja' or 'worship of instruments' and is an important part of the Navratris. This Hindu festival falls in the months of September or October in the Gregorian calendar, on the ninth day of the Navratris. On this day, weapons, instruments and tools by which one makes one's living are worshipped. Soldiers worship their weapons and artisans their tools. It is believed that praying with one's weapons or tools on this day invites divine blessings and helps one use these wisely. Sushil Uncle highlighted the symbolic nature of this festival.

In West Bengal, the ninth day of the Navratris is celebrated as Mahanavami or the day on which Goddess Durga killed the buffalo demon Mahishasura. In South India, Ayudha Puja celebrates the victory of Goddess Chamundeshwari over the demon Mahishasura. According to legend, after slaying Mahishasura, Goddess Chamundeshwari laid down her weapons, as there was no more use for them. The next day, which was Vijayadashami, celebrates her triumph over Mahishasura.

Sushil Uncle gave me some more details on this festival. He told me that three goddesses are worshipped during Ayudha Puja, namely Saraswati, the goddess of wisdom, literature and the arts; Lakshmi, the goddess of wealth, prosperity and abundance; and

Durga, the divine mother.

This day is also celebrated as Saraswati Puja, when children place their school books and pens in front of Goddess Saraswati and seek her blessings. So I took my books downstairs for the community puja and included my laptop as well. But I forgot to include my spatula. Next year, I'll definitely add it.

And before I forget, Sarla Aunty made two yummy Sindhi sweets for me: one was a meetha lola, a thick chapati made from wheat and sugar syrup. It was divine. She also sent me a plate of toshas, which were equally divine.

29

Dussehra Delight

'I declare in front of you all that on this Vijayadasami or Dussehra, I'll conquer my hatred of karela,' Sarla Aunty declared.

The Kapoors, Reema, Raunak, Lata and Pema were all spending the afternoon in the Sadhwani house. 'And I'll also conquer my fear of the camera.'

'Thanks to Chef Kunal Khanna's course, which was sponsored by Nikhil and Natasha, I've decided to innovate. I'll invent a dessert with karela, which will become everyone's favourite dessert.'

'Oh no,' Sushil Uncle groaned. Throwing an exasperated look at the twins, he said, 'Have mercy on me, don't ever send these two kitchen queens for such fancy courses. Now Sarla constantly wants to try fusion cuisines. She made chilli soufflé last week, and earlier this week, she made chutney biscuits.' Sushil Uncle rolled his eyes.

'Wait and watch,' Sarla Aunty said. 'This will be the best dessert you have ever eaten. I've decided to call it

Dussehra Delight. Like the world remembers Lord Rama's victory over the demon Ravana, they will also remember my victory over bitter gourd, the bitterest vegetable in the world.'

Sarla Aunty donned her apron and marched into her clean kitchen. Everyone followed her. She had bought a kilo of bitter gourd for the dessert.

'Nikhil, Raunak, start shooting, I want to upload the video online later,' she said.

The two boys pulled out their mobile phones and started recording.

'First, wash the bitter gourd well to remove all the mud from the ridges, then cut the top and bottom part,' she instructed.

Then, placing the washed vegetables on the counter, she made an incision along the length of each karela with the help of a sharp knife. Gently parting each karela so that it didn't split into two pieces, she scooped out the seeds to make the centre hollow.

After the seeds had been scooped out of all the bitter gourds, she laid them side by side on the counter.

'Now, I'm going to stuff all the bitter gourds with the mixture of dry fruit—crushed pistachios, cashews and almonds—and khoya, which I've already made,' she said.

After all the karelas had been stuffed, she put a big kadai filled with water on the gas stove and switched on the gas.

Then she added sugar to the water and let it boil. Soon, all the sugar had melted and the water began to bubble.

'I'll soak the stuffed karelas in this sugar syrup for six to eight hours,' she said. 'Make sure the sugar syrup is thin, so that it can easily penetrate the skin of the bitter gourd.' Turning to face the mobile phone cameras, she said, 'This is my innovation, which I've named Dussehra Delight. Before serving, I'll pour hot chocolate sauce over the karelas. I hope you all will like it.'

Everyone clapped. They all moved aside so Sarla Aunty could be the first to leave the kitchen.

After dinner, everyone gathered in the Sadhwani house.

They all watched as Sarla Aunty transferred her Dussehra Delight onto a long plate and poured hot chocolate sauce over it.

'Who wants to be the first to try my Dussehra Delight?' she asked.

All of them stared apprehensively at the dish, exchanging helpless looks as they tried to avoid Sarla Aunty's eyes.

Sarla Aunty's face fell when she saw their expressions.

'It's okay, I won't force anyone,' she said in a small voice.

'I would love to try your Dussehra Delight,' Nikhil volunteered.

'Me too,' Pema said.

With a thrilled expression on her face, Sarla Aunty cut one Dussehra Delight into two halves and served them both.

Nikhil hesitantly cut the dessert. Then, lifting a small piece, he shoved it into his mouth.

Everyone looked at him.

As he chewed, a dreamy expression came over his face. 'It's delicious,' he sighed.

'Can I have more?' Pema asked.

'You both like it?' Sarla Aunty asked.

'We love it!' they said together.

Everyone was served the innovative dessert, which surprisingly had shed all its bitterness and tasted delicious.

'Sarla, this is too good,' Dadi said between mouthfuls. 'Send the recipe to a contest.'

'I want to upload the video,' she replied. Turning to the boys she said, 'Please upload it now.'

Raunak uploaded the video right away.

A few minutes later, he announced excitedly, 'We have

already started getting views from all over the world.'

Within ten minutes, they had 300 views. By the following morning, both Sarla Sadhwani and Dussehra Delight had become a trending hashtag.

Natasha's Journal

If I tell you that we had a dessert made with karela today, you all will think I've gone mad. Sarla Aunty decided to conquer her dislike of bitter gourd, or karela, on Vijayadashami day, and she also decided to get rid of her fear of the camera. And she did both in style. She faced the camera like a professional, while making Dussehra Delight. Initially, I was scared to eat the dessert, but one bite and I was hooked. It was yummy!

Sushil Uncle told us that Dussehra, known variously as Dusshera, Dasara and Vijayadashami, is a Hindu festival that celebrates the end of the Navratris. It is celebrated on the tenth day and typically falls in the September or October months in the Gregorian calendar. He said that 'vijay' means victory and 'dashami' means tenth, so Vijayadashami.

Dussehra is observed for different reasons and is celebrated differently in various parts of India. In the eastern and northeastern states of India, it is celebrated as Vijayadashami, which marks the end of Durga Puja and celebrates Goddess Durga's victory over the buffalo demon Mahishasura and the restoration of peace, dharma and righteousness. The different aspects of Devi such as Durga, Saraswati, Lakshmi or Parvati are also revered on this day. In some places, people carry clay statues of Durga, Lakshmi, Saraswati, Ganesha and Kartikeya to nearby water bodies for immersion. They sing, dance and chant mantras along the way.

In the northern, southern and western states, the festival is called Dussehra, and the day marks the end of the Ramlila, which celebrates the victory of Lord Rama over the demon king, Ravana. Towering effigies of Ravana are burnt along with those of his brother Kumbhakaran and son, Meghnad, to symbolize the victory of good over evil. Sushil Uncle said it is believed that these effigies have a symbolic meaning: Ravana's desire to own another's possession, Meghnad's arrogance and overconfidence, and Kumbhakaran's insatiable hunger and laziness are inherent in each one of us. The burning of their effigies symbolizes the burning of our vices and negative qualities.

I am fascinated by the story of Ramlila. Sushil Uncle has agreed to take me for the Ramlila next year. I do hope I can see the burning of a Ravana effigy someday soon.

30

Diwali with a Difference

This was the twins' first Diwali in India. Both were excited to celebrate it.

'The children are up to some mischief,' Dadi said to her husband.

Putting down his newspaper, he snorted. 'You are always suspecting them of mischief.'

'I'm sure they are planning something,' she said. 'They haven't even started cleaning their rooms for Diwali.'

'Stop playing Sherlock Holmes,' Dadu said. 'It's their Diwali holidays; give them a break.'

'I can't bear this suspense!' Dadi stood up from the sofa and barged into Nikhil's room. 'Out with it,' she told the seven children sitting on the bed. 'What are you all planning?'

The children exchanged helpless looks. Nikhil and Natasha had taken Reema, Raunak, Pema, Amina and Arbaaz into confidence. Everyone agreed that it was a wonderful idea.

'Dadi, we have planned not to burst any crackers, as it is not good for the environment. In fact, we have all pooled some money and are planning to put together a goodie bag for the children of the slums,' Natasha said.

'We are making a list of the items we can put into the bag,' Reema added. She was holding a notepad in which she had made a list. A few items were scratched out.

'This is such a wonderful idea!' Dadi sat down on the bed. 'I'll contribute some money as well, and I'm sure so will your grandfather. Sushil Uncle and Sarla Aunty will also be happy to help, and Lata will not want to be left out either.'

'That will be great,' Amina said. 'That way we can also add an apple to the goodie bag. We were planning to put an eggless muffin, a packet of cream biscuits, chocolates, a packet of chips and a piece of mithai.'

Dadi brought her purse from her bedroom. 'Will five hundred rupees be sufficient?' she asked.

'Yay!' the children exclaimed in unison.

'I'll ask Ami and Abu to contribute too,' Amina smiled.

'I'll ask Mom and Dad too,' Pema added.

'I'm sure my grandparents will also want to be a part of this,' Reema said.

'And please clean your rooms,' Dadi told the twins, before leaving the room.

The other elders too loosened their purse strings. Soon the fund swelled, as did the number of items in the list.

'As Diwali is about lights, we can put in diyas as well,' Reema said, adding the item to her list.

'Instead of a single piece of sweet, we can make it a quarter kilo of mithai,' Pema spoke up. He had got over his initial shyness. 'That way, not just the children of the slums, but even their families can enjoy the sweets.'

'What a brilliant idea, Pema!' Natasha smiled.

Pema's face turned red.

'A superhero movie is releasing on Friday,' Nikhil said. 'Let's go for it over the weekend.'

'I won't be at home,' Reema said. 'I'm staying with my best friend as it's her festival after Diwali.'

'Oh,' Nikhil said. 'Which festival?'

'Chhath festival,' Reema replied.

Everyone looked at her with puzzled eyes.

'Let's finish with the goodie bag first, then I'll tell you about the Chhath festival,' Reema said, reading out the list they had made.

Natasha and Nikhil spent half the day cleaning their rooms.

'Gosh, I had no idea that I had so much stuff,' Natasha groaned as she sorted through the clothes.

'I'm tired,' Nikhil collapsed on his sister's bed.

It was decided that Sharbani Ma'am and Hetal didi would take the children shopping to buy the goodie bags and all the items. The children were divided into two groups;

one group went with Sharbani Ma'am and the other with Hetal didi.

'You bargain so well, Hetal didi,' Natasha said. 'Thanks to you, the shopkeeper reduced the price of the brown cloth bag from fifty rupees to thirty-five rupees.'

Soon, all the items were bought. The children started packing their goodie bags.

A day before Diwali—accompanied by Muniraju and Lata—they went around the slum to distribute the goodie bags.

'Thanks, Didi,' a small boy said, taking the goodie bag from Natasha's hand. She flushed with pleasure as no one had ever called her didi before.

'Thanks, Bhaiya,' a girl said shyly when Nikhil handed her the brown bag.

On Diwali afternoon, a few minutes before the auspicious time that the priest had given for Lakshmi puja, the twins trooped barefoot into the Sadhwanis' puja room along with Dadi, Dadu and Lata. Sarla Aunty had spread a clean bedsheet on the floor. In a large silver thali, she had kept silver idols of Lakshmi and Ganesha. Also in the thali were two silver coins, one with

the image of a swastika and the other with Lakshmi. All around the thali were small katoris filled with water, milk, curd, honey, rice, sugar, mithai, kumkum and flowers.

Everyone sat on the floor.

'Watch me,' Sarla Aunty instructed the twins. She first bathed Ganesha's idol with water, which she poured with paan leaves. Then, with a silver spoon, she poured a little milk, curd and honey over the idols, and placed rice, sugar, mithai and flowers at the gods' feet. After putting a dab of kumkum on Ganesha's forehead, she circled the diya before him. She then did the same for the idol of Lakshmi and the two silver coins.

After the rest of the elders had completed their puja, it was the twins' turn. Natasha and Nikhil followed Sarla Aunty's instructions.

The puja ended with Sarla Aunty's Lakshmi aarti.

After the puja, the children made a rangoli in the foyer of their building. Post sunset, they lit clay diyas all around the building.

'I'm so proud of the seven of them,' Dadi said to her husband. 'Nikhil and Natasha's mother wanted them to connect with their roots. But they have done more than that. They are imbibing the true essence of India's festivals and celebrations.'

Nikhil's Nook

Hi Friends,

I was thrilled when the girl who I handed the goodie bag to addressed me as bhaiya. Sadly, no one has ever called me bhaiya before, and I doubt Natasha will ever call me that either!

Dadi described the festival of Diwali. She said Diwali or Deepawali is one of the most popular Hindu festivals. It is celebrated on a no-moon day between mid-October and mid-November in the Gregorian calendar. Though the festival is celebrated in different ways across India, it symbolizes four different kinds of victories everywhere: of light over darkness, of good over evil, of knowledge over ignorance and of hope over despair.

Diwali is also called the festival of lights. 'Deepawali' means a row of lights. It is celebrated to mark the day Lord Rama returned to Ayodhya after completing fourteen years in exile. During this period that he, his brother Lakshman and his wife Sita spent in the forest, Sita was kidnapped and Rama and Lakshman defeated Ravana in Lanka. It is believed that Rama returned to Ayodhya on a no-moon night, or Amavasya. People lit diyas in their houses and all over the kingdom to welcome him.

Dhanteras is the first day of Diwali. Goddess Lakshmi and Lord Kuber are worshipped on this day to seek wealth and prosperity. The second day is called Naraka Chaturdashi. On this day, people have an oil bath to symbolize the washing away of the evil that might have attached to the human body in the form of dirt.

The third day is Diwali, when houses are decorated with rangolis and diyas are lit. Goddess Lakshmi is worshipped during Lakshmi Puja. It is believed that Goddess Lakshmi, the goddess of good fortune, wealth and happiness, roams the Earth on this day and enters clean and brightly lit houses. The fourth day is for Govardhan Puja and celebrates the defeat of Indra by Lord Krishna, when Krishna lifted the Govardhan mountain on his little finger, saving the people from Indra's rains and thunderstorms. On the fifth day, Bhai Dooj is celebrated, which is like the brother–sister ritual of Raksha Bandhan. It also marks the beginning of the financial year for businesses.

Sushil Uncle explained the reason people worship Lakshmi and Ganesha on Diwali.

According to legend, Goddess Lakshmi's arrogance about her power and wealth troubled her husband, Lord Vishnu, and he decided to do something about it. He told her that a woman is considered incomplete if she does not have children. Hearing this, Lakshmi appealed to Parvati to allow her to adopt one of her sons and assured her that she would look after him. Parvati allowed her to adopt Ganesha. Lakshmi then declared that whoever prayed to her for wealth, would have to first seek Ganesha's blessings. Sushil Uncle also added that since Ganesha is also considered the god of wisdom and Lakshmi the goddess of wealth and prosperity, worshipping both together means that one should not seek wealth without the wisdom to use it wisely.

In the run-up to Diwali, people clean, decorate and renovate their *houses and offices. On Diwali day, people dress up in new clothes and light diyas or candles in and around their homes and share sweets with family and friends.*

In the southern states, Diwali is celebrated as the defeat of Narakasura by Krishna. After defeating the evil king, Krishna freed the people imprisoned by Naraka.

I was so delighted to see the happiness on the children's faces. I hope we can do much more for them next year.

31

Making Karah Parshad on Gurpurab

'Dadi, where did you go so early in the morning?' Natasha asked.

'I went to the Gurdwara,' Dadi replied.

'I wish you had taken me with you,' Natasha said. 'I always accompanied Dad to the Gurdwara in Manhattan.'

'Next time, sweetheart,' Dadi said. 'Sarla and I went at around 5 a.m. I peeped into your room before leaving, but you were fast asleep. As I wanted to do seva, I didn't want to get delayed.'

'Oh,' Natasha said. 'Seva means service, right?'

'Yes,' her grandmother replied. 'I wanted to do seva for the langar.'

'What was your seva?'

'Making chapatis.'

'How many chapatis did you make?'

'I didn't count, but I'm sure they were in the hundreds,'

Dadi said. 'Do you want to help me make karah parshad?' she asked.

'I love karah parshad,' Nikhil said. The indigestion after the Onam gluttony was a distant memory. Nikhil had gone back to his food excesses, but he had also started playing badminton with Pema and Raunak in the building every evening after school and on the weekends, which he hoped would help burn off the extra calories.

'Any special occasion?' Natasha asked.

'It's Guru Nanak's Gurpurab today,' Dadi said. 'I usually make karah parshad and send it to everyone in the building. Want to help me?' she asked.

'Yes,' Natasha said. 'I'll be your assistant today.'

'Me too,' Nikhil followed his grandmother and sister into the kitchen.

Dadi placed a kadai on the gas stove.

'I've taken a little more than half a cup of ghee,' she said pouring the ghee into the kadai. 'Now I'll add one cup of wheat flour into it. Wheat flour doesn't need much ghee. Keep stirring continuously for three to four minutes over a medium flame so that

it doesn't burn, till the mixture turns brown and starts to give out a nice aroma,' she said, stirring with a steel spatula.

Soon, the kitchen was filled with the fragrance of wheat and ghee, and the mixture had turned an even brown.

'Now I'll add sugar,' Dadi said, pouring a cup of sugar into the mixture. 'Immediately after the sugar, I'll add double the amount of water into this mixture.' She poured two cups of water. 'On a low flame, I'll keep stirring until the flour absorbs all the water. See, it's done.' She switched off the gas and said, 'Karah parshad is ready.' She transferred it into a dish and covered it with a steel plate.

Carrying the covered dish into the puja room, she said, 'After my prayers, you can distribute it to the people in the building.'

Natasha's Journal

I've started to admire Dadi more and more every day. She is a perfect example of tolerance and harmony as she respects every culture and its traditions. She constantly says that there is just one god and all religions are just different means to reach god.

For Dadi, festivals are more about community celebrations, sharing one's blessings and enjoying yourself with family and friends.

Today, I helped Dadi make karah parshad for Gurpurab. Gurpurab celebrates the birth of Guru Nanak, the first Sikh Guru, and is also known as Guru Nanak's Prakash Utsav. It is one of the most sacred festivals of the Sikhs.

Dadi explained the significance of Gurpurab to me in detail. She told me that scholars believe that the founder of Sikhism, Guru Nanak, was born on 15 April 1469 on Baisakhi day in Rai-Bhoi-di Talwandi in the Shekhupura district of Pakistan, a place now known as Nankana Sahib. They also say that Guru Nanak was born on a full-moon day in the Indian lunar month of Kartik (October or November in the Gregorian calendar), which is the reason Gurpurab is celebrated in November and not in April.

Dadi said that Sikhs celebrate the birth anniversaries of all the ten Sikh Gurus. These Gurus formulated the tenets of the Sikh religion. She said that Gurpurab celebrations usually start with early-morning processions called Prabhat Pheris, which start from the Gurdwara and move through the surrounding areas. A forty-eight-hour Akhand Path, or a non-stop reading of the holy book of the Sikhs, the Guru Granth Sahib, is held in the Gurdwara two days before Gurpurab. The day prior to Gurpurab is for the Nagarkirtan, which is a procession led by the Panj Pyaras or the Five Beloved Ones. They carry the Sikh flag or the Nishan

Sahib along with the palanquin of the Guru Granth Sahib. The procession includes singers, brass bands, devotees singing hymns and the Gatka teams showing their martial-arts skills. The Gatka teams conduct mock battles using traditional weapons. The path of the procession is covered with banners, flags and flowers.

Dadi also added that she had participated in the Prabhat Pheris in her childhood along with her siblings. The leader of the procession spreads Guru Nanak's message.

These early morning processions can start as early as 4 a.m. This time of the day is called Amrit Vela, during which devotees sing Asaa-ki-vaar, a morning hymn. (Dadi said it was very exciting to be out of the house so early in the morning!) This is followed by a katha session, which is a reading from the scriptures, and an explanation of the significance of the morning hymn. After the katha comes the kirtan, or the session for the singing of devotional songs. The kirtan is followed by the langar. Dadi said the langar signifies that everyone should be offered food in the spirit of seva, irrespective of caste, creed or class, as everyone is equal in the eyes of god.

Dadi told us that when she was young, she would attend the night prayer sessions held in a Gurdwara close to her house with her grandparents. These prayer sessions begin around sunset, when the evening prayer called rehras is recited, followed by kirtan, which continues till late in the night. The congregation starts singing Gurbani at about 1:20 a.m., which is said to be the actual time of Guru Nanak's birth. The celebrations culminate at around 2 a.m.

I wish Dadi had taken me with her for the Gurpurab langar seva. Dadi said langars are community kitchens that are organized at the Gurdwaras by volunteers or kar sevaks. Though I may not have been of much help, I would have at least rolled out a couple of not-so-round chapatis. Well, next time I'll join Dadi and do proper seva for Gurpurab, and by then, I hope I'll be able to roll out rounder chapatis as well.

We missed Reema a lot when we went for the superhero movie during our Diwali holidays. While we were watching the capers of the superhero on screen, Reema was celebrating the Chhath festival with her best friend. Later, Reema told us all about the Chhath festival. She said it is an ancient Vedic festival of Hindus and is celebrated in Bihar, Jharkhand and Uttar Pradesh.

Reema told us that Chhath means sixth and is observed on the sixth day of the month of Kartik, which falls in the months of October or November of the Gregorian calendar. It is celebrated four days after Diwali.

Chhath is dedicated to the Sun God and is celebrated over four days. On the first day, people observing the fast bathe in a pond or river and eat a lunch comprising rice, dal and pumpkin. The second day is called kharna or kheer-roti, as the people eat kheer-roti for dinner after offering it to the Moon and to Goddess Ganga. On the third day, devotees fast without water and visit the banks of rivers to offer fruits and sweets to the setting Sun. On the fourth and final day of the festival, people pray and offer fruits and sweets to the rising Sun.

When we asked Sarla Aunty about Chhath, she gave us an interesting detail. According to her, in ancient times, rishis used the Chhath ritual to help them go without food for long periods of time, as by performing these rituals, they derived energy directly from the Sun.

Sarla Aunty has so much knowledge about festivals that my head reels with all the information she gives us!

32

Santas Come Visiting
on Christmas

'I can't believe that Dadi has not bought any Christmas presents for us,' Natasha told Nikhil after dinner on Christmas eve.

'I think she has forgotten our birthday too,' Nikhil said. 'Considering we share our birthday with Jesus Christ, it is difficult to forget the date.'

'She has completely avoided mentioning Christmas, even though she knows that in America, we always decorated a Christmas tree. I purposely mentioned it to her last week, but I don't think she was paying attention.'

'Have you spoken to Mom and Dad?' Nikhil asked.

'I spoke to them yesterday,' Natasha replied. 'Mom said that she and Dad will be busy today, but Mom promised to call us tomorrow.'

'Busy with what?' Nikhil frowned. 'I don't think they will be working during the holiday season.'

'I asked Mom,' Natasha explained. 'She said as she and Dad had to complete their projects soon to relocate to India, they were working during the holiday season.'

'That sounds fishy,' Nikhil said. Picking up his mobile phone, he dialled his Mom's number. Her phone was unreachable. He dialled his Dad's number. It was switched off.

'Strange,' he frowned. Looking at the wall clock, he said, 'It's 11:30 p.m. here on Christmas Eve. It must be the afternoon of the 24th in America now.'

Natasha's bedroom door creaked open. The twins were startled to see two people in Santa Claus outfits enter their room. Both the Santas carried sacks on their shoulders.

'Where is your stocking, child?' the thinner Santa asked. 'Hurry up, I need to visit other children too.'

'Where are my cookies?' the older Santa asked.

Jumping down from their beds, Nikhil and Natasha threw themselves at the two Santas.

'What a lovely surprise, Dad.' Tears filled Natasha's eyes.

'Dadu, I would recognize you anywhere,' Nikhil laughed, hugging his grandfather.

Their father and grandfather removed their Santa outfits and fake white beards.

The twins followed the elders out of the room into the hall where their Mom was decorating a small Christmas tree with gold baubles and a star. A large pile of presents lay next to it.

'Mom!' the twins hugged their mother.

At midnight, the door of Dadi's room burst open and she emerged. She was followed by Sarla Aunty, Sushil Uncle, Arbaaz, Amina, Lata, Raunak, Reema, Pema, Sharbani Ma'am and Hetal didi.

'Woof, woof,' Bruno streaked out of the room, barking excitedly.

'Happy Birthday!' the group, led by Dadi, screamed.

Their grandmother led them into the dining room. Two cakes—a chocolate cake in the shape of a badminton racket and a red-velvet cake shaped like a pair of ghungroos—sat on the long oakwood table.

'What a super surprise!' Nikhil ran towards his cake.

Dadi lit two small candles and inserted them into the

cakes. Handing them both a knife each, she said playfully, 'Now cut the cake together!'

Nikhil and Natasha cut their cakes to the offkey singing of the motley group of people. Then they ran around feeding everyone a piece of the cake. When Bruno was fed his share of the red-velvet cake, he wagged his tail in approval.

Lata cut slices from both the cakes and served them to everyone.

'We are coming to India for good in May,' their father said.

'That's super,' Natasha said and hugged her dad.

'And guess what? We have bought a flat on the second floor of this building,' their Mom said excitedly.

This news was received with cheers.

'I'm so happy.' Dadi wiped her tears.

Sarla Aunty sniffled into her handkerchief.

Dadu urged them all to move to the living room. The Christmas tree stood there with a pile of presents beside it. There were birthday and Christmas gifts for the twins. Everyone excitedly opened their gifts.

Nikhil's Nook

This is by far my best birthday and Christmas. I'm shocked that Dadi managed to plan this surprise without dropping a single hint. Dadi can certainly keep a secret! The best thing about celebrating our birthday on Christmas is that no will ever forget our birthday.

   Christmas is a Christian festival that marks the birth of Jesus Christ and is celebrated on the 25th of December. Mom told us the interesting story behind the birth of Jesus Christ. A young woman named Mary lived in a town called Nazareth a long time ago. She was engaged to a man called Joseph. One day, an angel called Gabriel visited Mary and told her that she would have a son named Jesus, who would be the son of God and saviour of the people, as he would save them from their sins. Around this time, the Roman emperor decided to take a census of the people. Like many others, Mary and Joseph arrived in Bethlehem for the census, travelling on a donkey. However, all the inns were full. A kind innkeeper, seeing that Mary was pregnant, allowed the couple to stay in the stable. Mary went into labour while they were in the stable and the baby was put in the manger. It is believed that after the birth of Jesus, on hearing from an angel that their saviour had been born, a group of shepherds rushed to the stable to see the baby. Around the time of Jesus' birth, three wise men—known as the Magi—saw a brilliant star in the sky over the place where he had been born. The wise men came to see the baby, bearing several gifts.

   Among the many traditions associated with Christmas is that of *completing the Advent calendar. For Christians, Advent is the time of waiting and preparing for the birth of Jesus at Christmas. It also marks his return at the second coming. The Advent calendar can be of different types and can even contain Christian poems and symbols, but its main aim is to count the days to Christmas. Some people also light the Christingle, an object that symbolizes Jesus Christ as the light of the world. Christingles are used both during Advent service and on Christmas. Other traditions include watching a nativity play, usually performed by children on Christmas, which recounts the story of Jesus's birth, and singing Christmas carols, which are Christmas-themed songs and hymns. Christmas trees are decorated with stars, baubles and lights. People greet friends and family and give them gifts and enjoy a Christmas feast together. They also go to church for midnight mass on Christmas Eve and for special services on Christmas day.*

One of my favourite Christmas traditions is decorating the Christmas tree. I also look forward to the visit of Santa Claus – a popular Christmas figure, also called Saint Nicholas or Father Christmas. It is believed that Santa—popularly represented as a plump man in red clothes with a flowing white beard and carrying a sack full of gifts—leaves gifts for children in the stockings hung near the bed or under the Christmas tree.

As everyone was so busy opening their gifts, I gobbled up three slices of cake. Hope I don't get a stomach ache!

Natasha's Journal

It's been a year since Mom and Dad dropped that bomb on us, saying that they had arranged for us to shift to India. Initially, I was scared whether I would adjust in India, or for that matter, whether I would get along with Dadu and Dadi (I had only met them twice before and for very short durations) and whether I would be able to cope in school.

Now, after living with them for nearly a year, I feel this was the best decision our parents made for me and Nikhil. I think it was great to get to know our grandparents and to make so many new friends – Amina, Arbaaz, Reema, Raunak and Pema. We have become so fond of so many different people here. At the top of my list are Sarla Aunty and Sushil Uncle, followed closely by Lata didi. Everyone has been so warm and welcoming. And I never thought I would like a teacher so much, that too a Maths teacher! But Sharbani Ma'am is truly the best and so is her friend Hetal didi. It was through these friends and family that I got a taste of India, its culture and its many festivals! Any wonder then that I decided to start writing a journal?

In fact, now that Mom and Dad will be back in India soon, I'll miss living with Dadu and Dadi. But luckily, as Dad has bought a flat in the same building, I've decided to spend my weekends with my grandparents.

ℰ Nikhil's Nook ℰ

This post is different from my usual posts about festivals. This post is about me and a year that began with my parents' decision to send us to India. My first thought was, 'How can they do this to us?' Within three days of being told about this move, we were on the plane to India.

All through my flight, I was grumpy, but something strange happened the moment I landed in India. My grumpiness disappeared, and within a few days, my irritation vanished completely. I think I adjusted faster than Natasha, though she will never admit it.

The one person who stands out for me amongst all the people we have met and been with in this last year is my Dadi. Although my Mom is a lot like her, I have never seen anyone as kind-hearted and generous as Dadi.

And although our parents did make us celebrate Indian festivals along with other Indian families while we were in America, it wasn't as much fun as it is to celebrate them here. And the food! The less said about that, the better. I think I have had a truly 'yummy' year, if I can call it that. And my blog was an attempt to record all the celebrations that went into making each festival special for us. I hope my blog posts did not bore you. Before I forget, Sarla Aunty has been offered a cookery show! I hope she agrees to host it.

Though I'm happy that my parents are shifting to India, I'm sad about leaving Dadi and Dadu. I've decided that I will stay with them during weekends. That way, I'll have the best of both worlds. And I'll also keep blogging, but I don't yet know what I'll write about. Do let me know if you have any suggestions!

RACHNA CHHABRIA has a fascination for words. She is at her happiest when she is writing stories and creating fantasy worlds for her books. Animal stories are her favourite. She is the author of *Lazy Worm Goes on a Journey*, published by Scholastic; and *The Lion Who Wanted to Sing* and *Bunny in Search of a Name*, both published by Unisun Publications. Her short story *Ganesha's Blanket of Stars* won the Special Prize in the Unisun-Reliance TimeOut Writing competition 2010–11. Her stories have been published in several anthologies and her articles have been featured in course books for schools. She is a regular contributor for many papers and a columnist with *Deccan Chronicle* and *The Asian Age*. Her children's stories appear regularly in *Young World*. She taught creative writing in a college in Bengaluru for many years.

RAYIKA SEN is a visual-communication designer based in Kolkata, India. She graduated from the prestigious Srishti School of Art, Design and Technology, and her primary interests include illustrating, designing, printmaking and experimenting with alternative storytelling methods.

ℰ ACKNOWLEDGEMENTS ℰ

Forever grateful to my dad, who continues to guide me from the unseen world and has been my motivation throughout my life. To mom, whose support is my oxygen, who patiently answered all my questions regarding festivals and customs.

To my Guru Amma (Sadguru Mata Amritanandamayi Devi), who is my constant source of strength and inspiration. To Ganesha, the original scribe, who steers my pen in the right direction.

To my family—Deepak, Jyoti, Anil and Kusum—thank you for all the love and support.

To Tina Narang, the best editor any writer can have. Thank you, Tina, for trusting me with this topic. This is the fastest book I've ever written. I could never have done this without your support, encouragement, suggestions and guidance. Our never-ending conversations and brainstorming sessions constantly threw up surprises.

To Rayika Sen, for her wonderful illustrations and for diligently following my illustration notes, so that the sketches match my vision.

To Nayantara Srinivasan and Ateendriya Gupta, for their meticulous proofreading.

To India, my beloved country, with its massive bouquet of festivals. It was an eye-opener researching for this book and learning all the customs and rituals associated with each festival and, of course, the mindboggling variety of food that forms a part of each.

A note of gratitude for all the people whose brains I picked while researching. It has been my endeavour to represent all the customs and rituals associated with festivals as accurately as possible.